Achilles Alexander Nobile

Miscellaneous Poems

Achilles Alexander Nobile

Miscellaneous Poems

ISBN/EAN: 9783337396671

Printed in Europe, USA, Canada, Australia, Japan

Cover: Foto ©Andreas Hilbeck / pixelio.de

More available books at **www.hansebooks.com**

MISCELLANEOUS POEMS

TRANSLATED INTO ENGLISH PROSE.

BY

A. ALEXANDER NOBILE, B.A.

Teacher of French and Italian.

MONTREAL:

WITNESS PRINTING HOUSE, ST. JAMES STREET WEST.

———

1884.

CONTENTS.

TRANSLATIONS FROM THE FRENCH.

TRANSLATIONS FROM THE ITALIAN.

I.

INFAMY.

TO REV. HATRLEY CARMICHAEL.

THREE families, hungry, naked, roofless; twelve
starved children, learning early in life how much
pity exists in human hearts, wandering on every road,
without finding shelter, stopped one day on that corner
of the earth which once was called Switzerland, the
hospitable.

At the sight of them suddenly anger is shown.
Rascals, vagabonds, beggars, away with you! Let us
cast on our neighbors this tiresome burden! Money-
less tourists come, out of the way! Off with you!
But neighbors, too, thank God, have police like us for
such visitors.

You have seen sometimes panting sheep, carelessly worried by butcher's dogs with hungry jaws,
bleating in despair, hurrying, pushing, and soon finding
no place to run to, to fly to, to escape this horrible torture, since on every side the teeth are ready to bite them.
And the butcher's boy joyfully chuckles, he hounds them
on, and "Bite him, there's a little one for you." It's

blood, it's flesh that the dog tears. It's an eye torn out that hangs on his jowl. It's a life in tatters; but close to the shambles its quicker work; and one gets through one's duty.

So the poor wretches cast on to the frontier twenty times are roughly repulsed. Pushed on and back, over marshes, down ravines, through forests, caught, let go, caught again, from night to dawn they go on, from dawn to eve they go on again. Oh, horror! in vain, with tears and cries the little ones shew the tormentors their mangled feet; in vain the rain drenches them, freezes them; no Christian offers them a place under his roof; no hearth for a moment warms the pale and fleshless bodies of these miserable ones.

Exhausted, they complain in a voice hardly audible, "Mother, I am hungry, cold; mother, my feet are bleeding; oh, mother, wait a little." But the orders are stern, Living or dead they must leave the country without delay. They must tramp, still tramp; and the police have many other cares, besides these cries and tears.

Drag them, beat them, if their spirits break down. No doubt the stick will restore their strength. Let us see how orders are carried out, and if to excel in this noble competition the zeal of different districts is unequal, so that we may give the prize to the most brutal.

When there comes to us, dragging on a useless life, some worn-out, wasted millionaire, well taught the respect due to money, we sniff them, and require nothing more; we pass him as respectable. and humoring his whims, we find a virtue in his every vice.

Scruples and morality we keep for the poor. Let us be proud of our hospitality; it is like a tavern dog, which humbly fawns on his master's customers, which loves good clothes, hates tramps, and always bites rags and licks velvet.

Poverty, poverty, how bitter is thy wrath, and what a crushing load is a burden of misery! Oh, mother of insults, what gall, what hatred, what fear, dost thou pour in thy long embraces, on those whom thou choosest, cleaving to them like a hideous leprosy, more deadly every day,

Never gaining a step, the poor man tramps day by day, wearing out his whole life to fight with famine, to add to the cares of to-day more racking than yesterday's, those of to-morrow, which wake him at night; unless, indeed, he spend the night in ruining his eyes in order that another may be amused, or glitter for an hour or two; to see his dear ones hopelessly languish in want; to suffer in their suffering; to have less rest than the cattle; and yet to dread losing a thankless labour, and in order to keep it to endure everything, contempt, hard words, from him who throws him a scrap of work.

That is his fate, and his mildest fate, too; that is what he is when he has food, when he is to be envied. Ah! now I understand knavery, cunning; the selling of soul and body to avoid such misery; every means being good to heap up money; for all is forgiven except the crime of an empty purse.

I feel myself shuddering with profound fear, for those who have bread, for the world's lucky men, when I see them teach the hideous lesson, that there is no room in the sunshine except for them, that for them grow the flowers of this human life, for others the thorns and endless woe.

Rich! open your eyes, it is now or never! there are noble hearts among you, I know there are, and pride has always saved me from envy, but most of you have only seen one aspect of life, only the laughing side of this two-fold world; ah! they would tremble to see the other.

Find a quick remedy for this eating evil! In prudence or in pity, come to help so many wretches whose groans, becoming every moment more distinct, are changing into cries, which, deaf that you are, the noise of your feasts cannot drown.

At least let fear loosen her fingers; sometimes after ball or concert, you throw into this bottomless pit alms which men applaud, and which fall like a drop of water in a huge conflagration; then, fools, you think you have satisfied this hungry crowd which grind their teeth.

Apportion, then, your balm to the horror of the wound. The workman, aghast at the future, must have a labor less thankless, so that he may think of his children, of his old age, without turning pale; he must live and must have some joy, some little happiness, which heaven sends you.

Hasten and weep for every moment! Some day death will come an unbidden guest to sit at your banquet. Then for the evil, which you have permitted, able to prevent it, on the earth, you, oh, ye rich, will answer tooth for tooth, eye for eye, body for body.

For him whom poverty drags into crime; for the maiden whom poverty defiles and throws into the abyss; for the cheat, the apostate, the groveller, the covetous; for all those whom famine ruins, the anger of God, taking shape before your eyes, will ask of each of you. "Cain what hast thou done with thy brother?"

In the name of earth and heaven help the poor. Keep a little money for his cup of wormwood. In your feasts, your balls, your games, let the memory rise that elsewhere some are desolate! Give, before is taken from you, for fear lest the flock, hunted by your hand, which bleats to-day, may roar to-morrow.

II.

A SUPPER OF KING ALBOINUS.

TO REV. J. R. DAVIS.

THE great mansion of King Alboinus was filled with sounds and songs, and amidst the dukes assembled at the meeting from every part of the kingdom, more than ever beautiful and happy, adorned with jewels and gold, was seated Rosmunda, chief ornament of this festival.

The cups with brims frothing with choice vines, pass round the banquet. Foaming liquor ascends to the head, and the king's eye, like his poniard, trembles and shines with a dark gleam. With laughter high and ferocious screamed the voices.

They spoke of our beautiful Italy, vanquished and oppressed by their swords, they praise these hills filled with so many vine trees. They, vile indeed, dare to call Italian women frail as flowers, rather than firm as pillars. They say all were gay, proud and beautiful, but servants. The charming Rosmunda, not yet used to the great crimes of this race, was sick at heart amid the noise of the horrid revel.

"Princes and barons, pages and knights, here is the most beautiful of my thoughts," (in the drunkenness of wine speaks Alboinus.) "Look at the woman who sits near to me so proud and so happy! who loves me so much! This is, indeed, the true jewel of my crown.

"Desirest thou dresses all embroidered with gold? Wilt thou have three hundred feasts and banquets every year? Italy is rich, very rich, truly; ask, and thou shalt have; but as all those valiant men in their castles must speak of thy virtues, and daily and nightly render jealous young girls and women, let them know all thy merits.

"That thou art good, Father Robert has preached it; that thou art chaste, I say it, and that is enough. Nimble of form, with small feet; that thou art beautiful, every one can easily perceive. Give them now a proof of thy courage;" and with a smile he offers her the naked skull of her murdered father.

"Come, Rosmunda, be strong, Rosmunda, drink. For me his blood, for thee, my vine; beautiful Rosmunda, such is the destiny. Thou hast kissed him before he died, kiss him now; and thou, departed King Gunimond, good day! Thou comest from the other world, here is the star of my family, kiss thy daughter."

The insult of the drunkard king pleased the guests, and was received by a boisterous, hellish laugh.

"King Gunimond, welcome! Where hast thou been? Why dost thou not take our hands? What has happened to thee? Thou hast lost thy eyes! O cursed knight, tell me something about the other life; then thou who knowest all, answer these two questions. Well fed, and without war, shall we remain long in this country? and on what condition will God give us this crown? White, mute and blind guest, kiss the rose near me. See how the poor maiden with pale face awaits thy kisses!" and so saying, the drunkard king played with the horrid skull, and quickly offered it to Rosmunda, who turned away her head.

"Stop, Alboinus, from thy lips do not ask such an infamous trial?"

"Drink, Rosmunda, not another word   I will it."

Rosmunda drank, but with her eyes seemed to say, Lombard King, if my revenge shall not fail, I will drink thy blood.

A year after this festival, the drunkard husband was sleeping alone. At night the beautiful Rosmunda opened her cell, and with a stalwart soldier, she had conspired to work his death.

Here at the dawn a soft knock was heard.—"Art thou Almachildes?"—"I am."—"What news bringest thou?" —"That the dead have a long sleep." And she, taking off the strong helmet of her knight. "This crown," she says, "my sweet, this crown sits better on thee. It was infamous; thou makest it honorable. Kiss me, and reign."

If I have narrated you a sad, iniquitous story, history cannot change. In the turbulent age, when Italy was a nursling, there happened many atrocious deeds, but at our epoch so polite and educated, husbands and wives, people and kings are all good.

III.

MONOLOGUE

OF

CHRISTOPHER COLUMBUS.

TO SIGNORE CAVALIERE GIANNELLI,
(Consul General of Italy in Montreal.)

I AM dying, old and wretched, and it was right that I should die in such a way! My life toiled through with suffering ends with grief; but amidst all God granted me so great and infinite a joy that every pain compared to it is a smile. God, who, when he pours on the world a ray of eternal light, recommends it to Italy, His beautiful Italy thus spoke to me, "Daring Genoese, try the sun's road!"

And I turned my eyes to the West, and I saw a new world, as it were, come out from the waves; immense forests of unknown trees, immense rivers, immense plains. There were the soft fruits which distant India ripens, which Europe envies and desires; birds, nameless with us, different wild beasts, seas filled with pearls, and mountains of gold,—and the voice said : " Go ; come back and tell the story." But I am poor ; sails do not spread at my command. I have nothing but a thought ! And I brought my thought to the crowned heads of the world and asked a little gold for recompense. Alas ! I was derided. For three long lustres I was scorned and went wandering, and nobody understood me. I heard not, I saw !

Here, bring me nearer to the balcony ; for pity sake do not take away from me the sight of the sea ! The sea ! the sea ! my kingdom, the friend of my youth and of my glory ! Let me greet it a last time and then let me depart for the journey from which no one returns.

I was so glad, so serene when, for the first time, I challenged it. Courageous, I pushed myself on its open bosom where man's eye never yet reached. Foolish cowardice imagined it to be filled with monsters and terrors. I was not afraid.

Fly, my ship ; if my heart beats it is not for fear of the waves, but for fear of my followers. Fly, fly my ship, let not mischevious omens arrest thy swift course. A new land is there. Gaily and speedily let us make sail for the foreign shore ; let us follow. God protects the bold undertaking. The wind is propitious, and the waves are gentle.

But already days go, months have passed away, and no trace of new countries is perceived. Our life is always between heaven and sea, and confidence has disappeared from every face. What more can I do to encourage those men who only understand the vile sound of gold ? I see other stars and other poles ! "Three days more, and if our hopes were vain, I surrender myself to you !"

Here we see flocks of birds rapidly fly from the West; sea-weeds and cleft wood from grounds not distant. Land ! land ! A panting cry breaks the eternal silence of the sky. It's the land ! It's the land ! Who could now describe my joy ? A light seen from afar in the dark air give strength to the assured heart and to the tired hand ! Forward ! forward ! Here is the dawn. Perhaps it is my dream. No, no, this is the longed for land, virgin, beautiful, dewy,—beautiful like a bride given as a reward to valour, fair and flowery like the hope courted by me for so many years. See the sun advance ; see the land smiles with proud life ! Furl the sails, lower the boat.— O, beloved land, at last I kiss thee ! O my ardent wished-for world, not in vain believed in by me, I greet thee.

The great work is accomplished ! Am I not now the master of my land and my sea ? Where is my royal palace? Where are my councillors, my jewels, my crown? Ferdinand, where is thy faith ?

Thou wast sitting proud in the conquered Alhambra, Granada lay vanquished at thy feet—a wandering Italian, burdened by thought, whom anguish had made old before his time, leading by the hand a little boy, came to thy throne. Around it were princes, lords, captains, and all Spain's ancient splendour. What, powerful king, on that day said the unknown Genoese ?

"Sire," he said, and he spoke without trembling, "fortune made thee sovereign of Aragon, love made thee master of Castille, war gave thee the beautiful kingdom of the Moors. Well, I will do for thee more than fortune, love, and risk of arms already have done, I will give thee a world!"

And then, O king, when from the far ocean unexpected I returned and brought thee gold and jewels of thy new kingdom, thine without a drop of blood shed, and to thy confounded sages and proud councillors highly I answered with facts, showing the proof of the glorious deed. What said'st thou, O king? Turning to thy subjects, thou didst exclaim, " Genius is a sparkle of the eternal idea, and is superior to every crown. Grandees of Spain, off with your hats!" Now I am the same Columbus. In the gold, the distant springs of which I opened, Europe swims and Spain is plunged to the neck. Poor and forgotten I beg my living crust by crust, and the discoverer of a new world has not a roof, nor a house where he may die in peace.

O, do not tell my grand-children such an infamy! O, do not say that these arms even yet keep the marks of chains, and that in the place of my triumph I lived a prisoner! Cruel story! If it was fated that such a recompense should follow the benefit, God be thanked, that I have not done it to Italy.

It was right, it was right; see the beautiful countries streaming with blood and with massacre. Of the people who butcher, and the people who suffer, which is the savage? Crime! Crime! The sword is plunged into the breast of innocent brethren, but this was not my intention when I undertook to guide you, ye wicked! It is not gold that tempts wickedness, but the vice is followed by useless offences ; these faithless men have made the Cross a pretext for butchery, the Cross, law of eternal pity. Cease, ye cruel, what rage maddens you ? Is gold not enough, that you wish even for blood ? And cannot blood quench your horrible thirst ? If this is valor what could be cowardice ! Shut out from my last moments this fatal scene ! Let me not see these horrors. Already high vengeance is moved, is awakened—it roars—it falls—and first on me.

It was right! ! it was right ! I bow my head.—O, sea ! The sight of thee is remorse to me. Though innocent we are accomplices in great disasters! Time will come when on blood and crime will rest the forgetfulness of centuries, and when from the new partnership will come to the universe as much good as formerly evil was produced ; then, amidst far posterity my name may be blessed, and a reward of honour more glorious because longer delayed may comfort my weary bones.

Now cover my face—I die in peace.

18

IV.

SAINT SILVESTER.

———

TO PROFESSOR DANIEL WILSON, L. L. D.,

(President of University College.)

———

THE year is departing. When a mere boy, ignorant of life, those days to me were so beautiful, and such holidays. Gaily with my soul full of hope I ascended those hard steps builded up with tombs.

The pride of being and of growing shone on my face; under my golden hair I showed myself a fair flowering shrub of which the living sap drinks and overflows in the sunlight.

If I counted the days, it was not for complaining of the days already past which had fallen as dead branches; without fear I could contemplate the future, and without remorse I could enjoy the present.

Far, very far from the ancestral hearth with void heart, mournful spirit, and broken body, forsaken amidst the swarming city, sad, depressed, martyrized, to-day the future frightens me.

To me it is like a dream, in which the pains of the day come back in turn to persecute us with human face, and without rest scourge us with love.

V.

THE NIGHT OF DECEMBER.

TO MY BELOVED SISTER,

Josephine Calligé, (née Sorvillo.)

AT the time when I was a scholar one evening I remained sitting up in the lonely hall, there came to sit at my table a poor child all dressed in black, who resembled me as a brother. His face was beautiful and sad; by the light of my lamp he came to read in my open book, leaned his forehead on my hand and smiling remained thoughtful until the morrow.

When I was fifteen years old I was walking one day with slow paces in a wood. At the foot of a tree came to sit a young man dressed in black who resembled me as a brother. I asked him my way; in one hand he had a lute, in the other a bunch of roses, he made me a friendly salute, and, turning himself, with his finger pointed to the hill.

I had reached the age at which we believe in love. One day I was alone in my room in the tears of a first sorrow. At my fire corner came to sit a stranger all dressed in black, who resembled me as a brother.   He was sad and thoughtful; with one hand he showed me the heaven, and with the other held a poniard.   It seemed that he suffered from my pains, but he did not sigh, and vanished as a dream.

At the age when man is licentious, one day I raised my glass to drink a toast at a feast; opposite to me came to sit a guest all dressed in black who resembled me as a brother.   Under his mantle he shook a rag of purple torn in pieces, on his head he had a wild myrtle, his thin arm tried to press mine, and the drinking glass in my feeble hand broke as soon as it touched his.

A year after in the night I was on my knees at the bed where my father had first died, there at the bedside came and sat an orphan all dressed in black, who resembled me as a brother.   His eyes were moistened with tears ; like the angel of sorrow he was crowned with thorns, his lute was lying on the ground, his purple was the color of blood, and his poniard was in his breast.

I recollected him so well that always in every moment of my life I recognized him.   It is a strange vision, and yet, angel or devil, I have seen everywhere his friendly shade.

When later, tired of suffering, I tried to exile myself from France to be born again or to die, when impatient of moving I went in search of the vestige of a hope, at Pisa to the feet of the Apenines,—at Koln opposite to the Rhine,—at Nice to the declivity of the valley,—at Florence in the midst of palaces,—at Brigues in those old

B

castles in the middle of the desolate Alps,—at Geneva under the cedars,—at Vevey under the green apple trees, —at Havre in front of the Atlantic,—at Venice on the arid Lido, where on the grass of a grave has just died the pale Adriatic ; everywhere over this immense earth I have wearied, and my eyes bleeding from everlasting wounds ; everywhere limping weariness, dragging my fatigue after it, has dragged me on a hurdle ; everywhere always thirsty for the knowledge of an unknown, I went after the shadow of my dreams ; everywhere, without having lived, I have seen what I had already seen, the human face, and its illusions ; everywhere I wished to live ; everywhere I wished to die ; everywhere I touched the land, always there came across on my path a wretched man, all dressed in black, who resembled me as a brother.

Who art thou, whom, in this life I have met in my way ? Seeing thee so sad, I cannot believe thee to be my evil genius ; thy sweet smile is full of infinite patience, and thy tears showed so great a pity. In looking at thee thy sorrow seems brother of my pain, and resembles friendship.

Who art thou ? Surely thou art not my good angel. Never thou comest to advise me. Thou seest my misfortunes, and strange to say thou indifferently dost let me suffer. For twenty years thou hast walked on my road, and until now I would not know how I should call thee. Thou smilest, without partaking of my joy. Thou pitiest me, without bringing me any consolation.

This evening also thou hast appeared to me. The night

was chilly. Alone, bent on my bed I was looking at a place, yet warm with burning kisses, and was thinking how soon a woman forgets, and felt a part of my life pine away.

I collected letters of past days, and tresses,—remains of our love. All this past repeated in my ears the eternal oaths of a day. I was looking at these holy relics which made my hand tremble. Tears of my heart, devoured by the heart, and which to-morrow will not be known, even from the eyes which have poured them.

I wrapped in a coarse covering the remains of happier days. Methought that here below what lasts longest is a lock of hair. Like the diver who goes down in a deep sea I lose myself in such forgetfulness. On every side I revolved the probe, and alone far from the eyes of the world I mourned o'er my poor buried love.

Already I was ready to seal in black those frail and dear treasures. Already I was to restore it, and not being able to believe it, I doubt it. Ah! feeble woman, proud, senseless, in thy spite thou wilt remember me. Why, why liest thou to thy own mind? To what purpose all this weeping, this swelling breast, these sobs, if thou dost not love me.

Yes, thou languishest, thou sufferest, thou weepest, but a dark shadow is between us. Well, then, good bye, adieu. Thou wilt count the hours which separate thee from me. Go, go, and in thy cold heart satisfy your pride. I feel my heart yet young and strong, and many evils could yet find a place upon the ill that you have caused me.

Go ! go ! immortal nature had not endewed thee with all virtues. Ah ! poor woman, who would be beautiful and not to forgive. Depart, depart, follow the destiny. I who love thee have not yet lost all. Throw to the winds our extinguished love. Is it possible ? Thou whom I loved so much ? If thou wilt go why lovest thou me ?

But suddenly in the darkness of night I see a form cross the room without making noise. I see on my curtains appear a shadow ; it came to sit on my bed. Who art thou, pale face, sad portrait of myself dressed in black? What wilt thou, wicked bird of passage ? Is it a dream ? Is it my own image that I see in my glass ? Who art thou, ghost of my youth, pilgrim whom nothing could tire? Tell me why I find thee on the shadow everywhere I go. Who art thou solitary visitor, assidous host of my pains ? What hast thou done to be condemned to follow me on the world ? Who art thou, who art thou, my brother who appears to me only on the days of sorrow ?

THE VISION.

Friend, my father is also thine. I am not the guardian angel, neither the evil genius of men. I do not know where are directed the steps which I love in this little world in which we are.

I am not God, neither devil, and thou hast called me

with my name when thou hast called me brother. Where thou wilt go I will always follow till the last day in which I will go to sit on thy grave. Heaven has entrusted thy heart to me. When thou sufferest come to me without inquietude ; I will well come after thee on the road, but I cannot touch thy hand, friend ; I am

THE SOLITUDE.

VI.

DANTE.

TO THE HON. JOHN BEVERLEY ROBINSON,

Lieut.-Governor of Ontario.

La colpa sequirà la parte offensa,
In grida come suol.

—DANTE.

IT was evening. Deprived of its magnificence the sun now arrived at the dimmed horizon, was departing silently, without strength, like an exiled king, who passes away unknown. Upright upon a hill whence Florence could be seen, leaning on his sword still unsheathed and bloody, a soldier, fierce in the face, yet dusty from the battle scarcely ended, all of whose companions were flying at random, stood casting on the distant city a long and painful look. A deep sigh heaved his breast, his eye sparkled, and his voice made the hill tremble.

" Vanquished! exiled like a brigand! driven away by the fate of the battlefield! without even having the fortune to die fighting beneath our walls! Vanquished! From valley to valley to drag along my sad life, begging from half-hearted friends!—to eat the hard bread of alms until my last hour comes! These are the rights I have won !"

" I must fly, then, far from thee, dear and ungrateful city,—live and suffer far from thee without hope ! Of all the misfortunes which from this moment will weigh on me, the greatest will be never to see thee again. Thou sun, who art dying, continue thy course and enlighten still the roof of my ancestors, and the holy place where under the black stone are sleeping in peace my mother and my father. Oh, why could I not sleep near them ! Thou belovèd Beatrix, who scarcely hast touched our world while directing thy course toward heaven, in thy great glory dost thou still remember thy friend ? Vision so short and so beautiful ! Oh, bright day, what was thy to-morrow ? Watch over me, radiant immortal one ! Sweet-eyed angel, cover me with thy wings ! Happy star, point me out my way ! "

Dante was silent, and as in the tempest the oak tree lowers the pride of its branches, the exile bent under the burden of his misfortunes, lowered his face, and with tormented soul, and with eyes full of tears, tasted long the bitterness of his pains. A noise came to draw him from his thoughts,—a noise feeble at first, but continually increasing ;—a terrible mixture of saddened bells, of a nation's curse, of songs of victors, and of cries of the vanquished.

This noise was the uproar of the people of Florence. Humbled on account of their fears, to feast their victory they asked for vengeance, and without pity dragged to the scaffold many prisoners spared by the sword in battle.

Like a lion awakened by a sudden noise, which, with

flashing eyes rises and pricks his ears, the soldier started
at the words which reached him with the echo, and coming out from his sad rest, for a moment listened to the
brutal orgies ; and then, with his arms extended toward
his native city, thus addressed her :

".Senseless populace ! Go on ye, who curse the sacrificed, and only help the strongest! Join death to thy
pleasure. Mingle blood with the vine of thy feast.
Laugh at the execution prepared for those who, moved
by fate, have risked their life for thee !

"Go on with thy work, and hasten. Canst thou, in
thy wisdom, know how many hours are needed to change
joy into dread, and grief into joy,—how long lasts so
sweet a power,—and if the oppressed remain long on
, their knees ?

" Without doubt, puffed up by their fortune, triumphant and full of bitterness, the *Neri* already say, ' Our
reign is sure ! ' Thinking this reign an easy task, and
the league of the *Bianchi* crushed, they strike our rem-
nant, and scoff at us with jest and sarcasm.

" Oh, *Neri*, know how to maintain yourselves kings of
the present. I have the future, and you, I dare to think
will follow me thither. Ungrateful history may leave in
darkness your great exploits. I, in this terrified world,
just towards so great a glory, will immortalize you.

" Pouring infernal light on your venal spirits, I will
pourtray you to future ages, and will discover the nig-
gardliness, the jealousy, the treachery, the hypocrisy of
your hearts, and upon your soiled names will throw tor-
rents of terrible verse. Oh, inconstant and deceiving

people! I feel the day of vengeance coming! Tremble! I see the supreme wrath, bend thyself under its curse, misfortune break thy pride, every hour will bring a new pain, and thou wilt torture thyself as a man alive in a tomb."

The night had come. A blast of tempest roared passing through the air; the dark heaven was reddening, and the arm of the sad prophet seemed to threaten the perverse, and the inspired forehead of the divine poet was surrounded by lightning.

From nation to nation, from place to place, untamed, uneasy, full of hatred and love, the great outlaw wandered twenty years, far from his town, always dreaming of his return.

Until the last hour he nourished the hope of seeing this happy day. Death only took pity on his long sufferings; and the old Ghibelin never more saw Florence,—which has not even his tomb* within her walls.

---

* Since the poet wrote these verses, Florence has acquired the remains of her immortal though despised poet. — *The Translator.*

VII.

HOPE IN GOD.

———

TO J. DUNFIELD, ESQ., M. D.

———.

AS long as my feeble heart, yet full of youth, shall not have bid farewell to its last illusions, I would abide by the old wisdom which has made a demi-god of the sober Epicurus. I would live, love, accustom myself to my equals, go in search of joy without relying upon it, do what has been done, be what I am, and carelessly lift my eyes to heaven.

It is impossible. Infinity torments me. In spite of myself I cannot think of it without fear or hope, and notwithstanding all that has been said, my reason is frightened at seeing it, and not being capable of understanding it. What is this world? and what have we come to do in it, if to leave in peace it is necessary to veil heaven? To pass like sheep with our eyes fixed on the ground and to forsake all else, can that be called happiness? No, it is to cease to be a man, and degrades the soul. Chance has put me in the world. Happy or unhappy I am born of woman, and I cannot throw off humanity.

What can I do then ?   " Be merry," says paganism, " be merry and die ; the gods think only of sleeping."

" Hope," answers christianity, "heaven always watches, and thou canst not die."

Between these two roads I hesitate.   I should wish to follow a more easy path, but a secret voice tells me that there is none, and that with regard to heaven one must believe or deny.   This is my opinion too.   Tortured souls cast themselves, sometimes in one, sometimes in another, of these two extremes   The indifferent are atheists,—if they would doubt only for a day, they could not sleep. I yield, and as matter leaves in my heart a desire full of dread, I will bend my knees, I wish to believe and to hope.

Here I am in the hands of a God more dreadful than all evils of this world put together.   Here I am alone, a wandering, weak and miserable creature beneath the eye of a witness who leaves me not.   He watches me, he follows me.   If my heart beats too quick I offend his dignity and his divinity.   A precipice is opened under my steps.   If I fall into it to expiate an hour, an eternity, is needed.   My judge is a tyrant who deceives his victim. For me everything becomes a snare and changes its name. Love becomes a sin, happiness a crime, and all the world is for me a continual temptation.   I have nothing more of humanity about me.   I await the recompense, I try to avoid the punishment, fear is my guide, and death is my only aim.

Nevertheless, it is said that an infinite joy will be the share of some elect. Who are those happy beings? If thou hast deceived me, wilt thou again give me life? If thou hast told me the truth, wilt thou open the heavens? Alas! this beautiful country, promised by thy prophets, if it really exists, must be a desert. Thou requirest those chosen to be too pure, and when this happiness arrives they already have suffered too much. I am a man, and I will not be less, nor attempt more. Where should I stop? If I cannot believe in the priest's promises shall I consult those who are indifferent?

If my heart wearied by the dream which troubles it returns again to reality for consolation, at the bottom of the vain pleasures called into my aid I find a disgust that kills me. In the same day in which my thoughts are impious, in which to end my doubt I wish to deny, even though I possessed all that a man could desire, power, health, wealth, love, the only blessing of this world, though the fair Astarté worshipped by Greece should come from the azure islands, and should open her arms, though I could come in possession of the secret of the earth's fertility, and thus changing at my fancy living matter, create a beauty for myself alone, though Horace, Lucretius and the old Epicurus seated near me, should call me happy, and those great lovers of nature should sing the praises of pleasure, and the contempt of the gods, I would say to all, " In spite of our efforts I suffer, it is too late, the world has become old, an infinite hope has crossed the earth, and against your will, we must raise our eyes to heaven."

What other should I try? Vainly my reason tries
to believe, and my heart to doubt. The christian affrights
me, and in spite of my senses I cannot listen to the
atheist's persuasiveness. Religious people will call me
impious, the indifferent will call me a fool. To whom shall
I address myself, and what friendly voice will comfort
my heart wounded by doubt.? It is said that there exists
a philosophy which can explain everything without reve-
lation, and which in this life would guide us between in-
difference and religion. Granted. Where are those makers
of systems who without faith know how to find the truth?
Weak sophists, who believe only in themselves, what are
their arguments, what their authority? One show us
two principles at war with one another, which alter-
nately conquer, both being everlasting.*

Another, far away in the desert, heaven discovers a
useless God, who will not have any altar.† I see Plato
dreaming, and Aristotle thinking. I hear them, I praise
them, but I pursue my way. Under absolute kings I
find a despot God, now they talk of a republican God
Pythagoras and Leibnitz transfigure my being. Descartes
leaves me perplexed. Montaigne after great examination
cannot understand himself. Pascal trembling tries to escape from his own visions. Pyrrho blinds me, and Zeno
makes me insensible. Voltaire throws down all he sees
standing. Spinosa tired of trying the impossible, vainly
searching for his God, ends by seeing him everywhere.
With the English sophist‡ man is a machine, finally from

* Manichean.   † Theism.   ‡ Locke.

the fogs comes a German* rhetorician who, finishing the ruin of philosophy, declares the heaven empty and proves that there is nothing.

These are the wrecks of human science, and of her five thousand years continually doubting, after such a great and persevering work here, one finds the results at which we have arrived. Poor foolish, miserable brains, who have explained all in such different ways, to reach heaven you needed wings. You had the desire but faith was not with you. I pity you; your pride came from a wounded soul, you have felt the pains which my heart suffers, and you well know this bitter thought which has made man tremble whenever he considers infinity. Well, come on, let us pray together, let us abjure the misery of your childish calculations of such a vain work. Now that your bodies are dust I will pray for you on your graves. Come pagan rhetoricians, masters of sciences, christians of old times, and thinkers of the present age, believe me, prayer is a cry of hope. Let us address ourselves to God in order that He may answer us. He is just, He is good, without doubt He forgives you. All of you have suffered, the rest is forgotten. If heaven is a desert we shall offend nobody; if there is One who hears us, may He pity us.

PRAYER.

O thou whom nobody has been able to know, and

---

* Kant.

whom none could deny without lying, answer us, thou
who hast made me, and to-morrow may makest me die.
Since thou lettest us understand thee, why, at the same
time makest us doubt thee ? What sad pleasure canst
thou feel in tempting our good faith ? As soon as a man
raises his head he thinks that he sees thee in heaven, all
creation in his eyes is only a vast temple. If he descends
into his inward thoughts he finds thee, thou livest in him.
If he suffers, weeps, or loves, it is his God who had so
willed. The noblest intelligences apply their most sublime
ambition to prove thy existence and in teaching thy
name. Whatever is the name which is given thee, Brah-
ma, Jupiter or Jesus, true eternal justice, all arms are
extended to thee. The last of the sons of the earth thanks
thee from the depth of his heart as soon as to his misery
is added a simple appearance of happiness. All the
world glorifies thee; the bird from its nest sings to thee;
and thousands have blessed thee for a drop of rain.
Nothing has been done by thee that is not admired; none
of thy gifts is lost to us; all pray; and when thou smilest
all bend the knee before thee. Why, then, supreme Master, hast thou created evil so great that reason and even
virtue tremble at the sight ? Whilst so many things in
the world proclaim the divinity, and are witnesses of
the love, power, and kindness of a father; how is it that
under the holy sky are seen actions so shocking as to
check the prayer on the lips of the unhappy ? How is it
in thy divine handiwork are so many elements not in
harmony ? To what purpose are pestilence and crime !
Just God, why death ? Thy pity must have been great

when with all its good and evil this marvelous and beautiful world emerged from chaos! Since thou wouldst submit it to the pains of which is replenished, thou oughtest not to have permitted it to discern thee. Why lettest
thou our misery see thee and guess a God? Doubt has
brought desolation on the earth, we see too much or too
little. If thy poor creature is too unworthy to approach
thee, thou oughtest to have let nature veil and hide thee.
Thy power would have been left to thee, and we should
have felt its blows; but quiet and ignorance would have
lessened our evils.

If our afflictions and pains reach not to thy majesty,
keep thy solitary grandeur, shut forever thine immensity
but if our mortal griefs come to thee, and from the eternal plains thou hearest our laments, in grace break
then the deep vaults which cover the creation, lift this
world's veil, and show thyself a just and good God!
Thou wilt see all over this earth an ardent love of faith,
and humanity will fall down before thee. The tears
which have exhausted him, and which flow from man's
eyes as a light dew will disappear in the heaven. Thou
wilt hear only thy praises, and a concert of joy and love,
like that which the angels gladden thy heavenly kingdom,
and in this supreme *Hosanna* thou wilt see at the sound
of our songs doubt and blasphemy fly away, while death
itself will join its accents.

VIII.

MARK BOTZARIS,

TO SIR W. P. HOWLAND, C. B., K. C. M. G

I.

HALF a century has already passed since the day in which, tired at last of the intolerable yoke, all the untamed Greeks upraised their bent heads and unsheathed their swords, surging to the dangers of unforeseen struggles, but inly too joyful in the attempt to deliver their country from the horrors of slavery. Europe was astonished at the strange news, but ere long Britain, France and Italy sent their sons to the defence of the sister who was hesitating in the dangerous clutches of the Islamic panther, and removed the yoke imposed on Athens by Constantinople. The blades glittered in the sunlight, and new Alexanders they cleft the Gordian knot and gloriously made their brethren free. Of this holy war and of the memorable deeds sung of the brilliant champion hero

c

and supreme chief, who as in the sky shines the sun superior to all, shines for our inspired poets.

Let me, O, intrepid hero, sing a song in thy memory
about the ever glorious day in which thy country was
preparing her courageous sons for the defence of her brethren who were yet groaning, a prey to the Ottoman's,
and impatiently waiting for freedom to be extended over
all Greece. The day is near, I hope that the Muscovite
will destroy the haughty Mussulman. The bells ring, the
cross rises, and the crescent lowers, like the owl at the
breaking of day flies from rock to rock. Hope, O, Grecians! this day is near; already I see around me unfolded in the air the avenging standard of the Christians;
already I see the Soliman fall suppliant. Rise, O, glorious
country, dear to God! This is the thought of the people,
and this is my hope! and while to Botzaris I begin to
sing my sincere verse, inspire thyself with the holy ardour
which burns in me, and let the world admire thee, while
loud plaudits will crown the success. Do not hesitate,
rise up! What carest thou for ruins, if in the Neropolis
thou canst see die him, who once crushed, but always despised thee?

II.

It was already time when Hellenia, torn piecemeal, lay a
prey to the Ottoman hyena. The terrible ravaging sword
of Mahomet had rent into a thousand pieces the ancestral
land, nest of glory and of great virtues, and without fear
had enslaved the offspring of Sophocles and Lycurgus.

Separated from the other sisters Hellenia alone was not enough for such an enemy, and Athens—conquered. forsaken and tired succumbed, to the will of Soliman.

O, how many and what awful arts the victors employed toward the conquered ! O, who will give me strength to narrate the infinite tears poured out by Epaminondas' sons, once great, now conquered, and at the will of a cruel destiny ? The most beautiful of the Hellenian maidens, the most chaste wives, innocent girls of scarce ten years were condemned to the vilest wishes of their master, who to watch over them employed iniquitous, wretched eunuchs, (scorn and horror of the world) hideous, but made yet more vile and ferocious by reason of their lost manhood, and the continual tortures to which they are condemned, forced to watch those near whom they lose their reason. Husbands, parents, sons, children, beseeching matrons, all were slaves. The once rich but now all ravaged fields were made haunts of wild beasts and caverns of horrors. The power of the right and of reason was lost, and the few spared by cruel fate, lay spiritless and annihilated on the ground. Justice slumbered and always was deaf to the querulous voices of the thousand afflicted who implored her. Hope was dead. Everywhere the abject crescent shone unjust and atrocious. But one day from heaven, like a summer's ray, which after a long rain fills with life the languid flowers, descended an elect who, after long study of the wounded country, and afflicted humanity, felt an intense horror for his suffering country, and daring soon destroyed every seed of incertitude. Turning his looks to this land, which

once so rich in virtue and great exploits, was the model
of great enterprise. "Let us not, he says, let not longer
endure this abominable condition which presses us! Are
we not sons of God? Why have we an heart? How
could we look silently at the slaughter around us, and not
feel a holy wrath, which impels us to seize our arms and
to reinflict on the oppressor's head the same griefs? The
Almighty give us strength and manly hands able to
avenge our injuries. Up, then, sons of Greece! I spur
you to freedom, to freedom which smiles on us. In the
name of God, who now inspires me; in the name of the
suffering which grieve you; in the name of our suppliant
daughters exposed to the filthy kisses of the tyrant; in
the name of our glorious ancestors, I, a son of Hellenia,
invite you to revenge. We are few, 'tis true, but we are
resolute and loved by God. Look how there the Saviour's
cross flaps in the blue sky! Let her be our guide, O,
Grecians, and let us conquor."

III.

The tyrant is fallen! The thousand cohorts of the
cruel oppressor so dread before, fall now in the dark sojourn of death. Hellenia already is awakened from her
long sleeping. Thousand, many thousand are those valiant ones, who march through the field of glory, inflicting
the terrible anguish of prolonged suffering. Impelled
by a heavenly sacred spark they march ready to bring
death, or to die. The immortal genius of Botzaris already

shines, already the conquered bands of the Mussulman flee. Dispersed through the fields they go begging for peace, falling, moaning, imploring mercy. The crescent is destroyed, and the wicked blood of the conquered runs in streams. The Grecian are victorious, but this victory is dearly bought. The hero of the heroes faithfully unfolding the cross, exciting his followers to bravery, fighting himself bravely, is wounded and near to death.

Everywhere rise cries of grief, and the eyes of the valiant are moistened. The bold and mighty leader is dying mortally wounded. The hero weeps not, but turning his eyes to heaven implores its pity for his dear countrymen.

"Destiny is accomplished," thus he spoke, "and I depart to the bosom of the everlasting where grief is unknown, but at least I see you free before I go. Alas! I faint at such a joyful thought. Death smiles on me because I die the same day Hellenia has been able to break her fetters. —Beautiful it is to die free on the field—for one's fatherland—Greeks I leave you—receive my last farewell....."

Thus spoke the warrior, and while the air resounds with his words joined with the echo of the martial guns, the oppressor was in flight, and sad sad on the ground already reddened with the outpoured Ottoman blood was deposited the dead body of Mark, the chief and the victor.

Kneeling the soldiers prayed, and their prayers went to the Almighty in company with his dying soul. He accepted favourably those prayers and mercifully watches o'er Greece. The lamented hero avenger of his land lives and will live in the heart of the present and every future generation as a rare example of love to one's country. Ye Greeks, remember Missolunghi, and arise!

IX.

CHARITY.

TO REV. D. J. MACDONELL.

WHEN the pining flower that summer causes to fade leans toward the burning soil to die, and to quench the fire by which it is devoured, asks and begs only a drop of water; without rain or dew this dying complaint fell with the wind's breath.

So when the unhappy drags himself alone, bent from the cradle under troubles, oppressed by his burden, if the arm of his brother does not support his misery, if some sweet voice does not speak him a word which raises and comforts, he must fall under the weight.

O, sublime charity, balm of grief, thou whose sight inspires courage, thou who driest tears; beloved daughter of God! Pain and bitter complaint are silent before thee; peace is in thy mouth, and those touched by thy hand suddenly lose their fears.

He who lost in doubt and in despair since long has strayed from the right path, by thee is brought repentant to God whom he had forgotten, and thou restorest hope in him who hoped no more.

O, Supreme Majesty, thy sovereign order has said "Love thy neighbor as thyself." The man only to whom misery never is troublesome is just in thy eyes. If on earth he is poor, by the good action he has done he will become rich in heaven.

X.

THE TWO MOTHERS.

TO HON. CHRIS. S. PATTERSON,
Judge of the Court of Appeal.

"I must go, and must take away from thine arms,
O poor wretch, this my darling, who has made thee so
happy."

I.

ON the river Loire which, like a silver thread, runs over a hundred miles of happy land, proud and gay the citadel of Saumur raises its head.

Like fresh beauties bathing themselves in the sea, her white houses extend along the river, half naked and half masked by vineyard and roses. Neither hot nor frost. It is an eternal spring. O, yes! beautiful and cheerful is the citadel of Saumur.

And there near the walls like a soft pillow is a gentle descent with its mantle of verdure and the shadow of its avenues. But this verdure, and these flowers are not a complete paradise, and mixed with such a celestial smile is a house of sorrows.

Yes, a mad-house is at the bottom of the avenue.
Amidst the silence of the nights, amidst the gloomy wings
of the wind are heard interrupted plaintive and deep
sounds of lament, merry songs or strange voices, blasphemies and atrocious laughs.

And a strong feeling, of which nobody dares to ask the
reason, forces every person to pay a visit to this living
churchyard.

II.

On the last hour of a splendid sunset a beautiful young
lady, giving her hand to her little daughter, ascends the
hill.   How charming was the little angel of five years,
dressed in white, fresh, smiling, handsome and nimble.

The shining and fair hair descends on her shoulders
like waves, and with her provoking looks call for kisses.
" Mother, can you tell me how these poor madmen live ?
O ! how anxious I am to see them ; mother, come."

The door is open, they ascend two stairs, they are in
the asylum court.   It was the time of the daily walk, the
hour of gaiety.   One heavily walks, another recites, and
another sings.   Some jump up and down, some sit on the
ground and others laugh.

A woman with loose hair and a dark petticoat, alone,
far away in a corner, sits on a bench as if tired by long
work.   On her pale cheeks there is an old trace of tears.
She turns around her stupid and dull glazed eyes.

God had given her as a token of a first love a girl,

whose face was as beautiful as that of a cherub. How
she did love her dear daughter, how she watched her
white cradle ! Holy and deep affection ! For this happy
mother her girl was the world. A cruel illness had stolen
this gem of her life, and heart-broken from the great
sorrow she became mad, and for five years the poor wretch
waited for her darling, and asked of all, if they had seen
the lost one. Everybody who saw her with this intense
pain engraved on her squalid forehead feels in his own
soul a charm forcing him to tears. The kind lady approached near the unhappy mother, probably moved by
such a great sorrow.

Clinging to the skirt of her dress her little daughter
thrusts forward her head, and with her eyes filled with
tears, she says, " Poor thing ! " Then softly approached
to the mad woman and with her little hand caressed her
dark hair.

Shaken at this touch the unhappy one turns a look to
the little angel, and a strange flash shines in her eyes
then fixedly looking at her, she uttered a cry, opened her
arms, and with an impetuosity of affection pressed to her
breast the little one.

" O, my daughter, my dear daughter, how strong is this
joy which overflows my heart ! Almighty God, let me die
in such a happiness ! Die ? Who speaks of death ? To
live, I say yes, I will live now that I have found thee,
and I will live always near to my child.

" Come, sit here on my knees, let me kiss thy beautiful
eyes, let me forget these few years of horrid anguish.
From the very first day I lost thee, my eyes had no more

tears, but the excessive ecstacy of this hour makes me weep anew.

"Tell me, where, where thou hast been all these years I was in search of thee ? Hast thou perhaps been in the joy of the other life ? But even in heaven in vain thou hast asked my sweet kisses, and now thou comest back to the loving embraces of thy mother. Thou comest now and will fly no more from these arms. I would rather die, O, yes, I feel that surely I would die, if again thou wert taken away from me."

III.

In such way she spoke and convulsively pressed the girl to her panting bosom, and in the intoxication of her deluded affection kisses without number came from the burning lips. It was a fever of infinite love that sweetly melted her heart. The dear girl with her little hand carressed the dark hair, and in return kissed the unhappy woman and smiled at her with love's smile, the young mother not daring to trouble the joy of such a brief enchantment.

In the meantime the falling evening's twilight was shedding its pale light, and the dread band of guards opened the door of the inner staircase, the clock of the asylum calling the family of lunatics to their respective cells. The kind stranger who feared to destroy the joy of this holy mistake approached near the poor mad woman, telling her in a pitiful voice of love, " I must go, and I must take away from thy arms, poor wretch, this, my darling, who has made thee so happy!" Jumping up the mad woman with ferocious fear pressing the girl to her breast, "Who art thou, she cried to her with harsh voice, who comest to trouble my motherly affection?

"Knowest not thou that neither Satan nor God could ravish me of my little angel? Away, far from me. Woe to him who will dare to touch only a hem of her dress. Rather than permit her to be taken away from my arms, I would rather she should die, O, yes, I will kill her rather than lose her again—"

Neither prayer nor threat could subdue the delusion of her mind, and with her lean arm raising the little girl, if any one came forward, only a step, she meant to throw her on the ground, and such was the strong resolution shining from her gesture and from her accents, that it was thought better to leave her alone, and to await the events of the night.

Therefore all retired, and she with the girl ran into her cell, and there in haste putting in order the bed lay in it her child, and arranging with care the folds of the rough sheets, joyfully sits at the bedside looking at her, smiling and kissing her.

Under the pressure of the hand which softly caresses the girl, she shuts her large eyes, and yielding to the weariness and sleep fell into a sweet slumber, whilst the mad woman who was near to her soothed her repose with this song:

"Sleep, girl, my jealous eye as a guardian angel watches

at thy placid pillow, and the interminable kiss like music sooth thy slumbers.

" Sleep, darling, and let me see the moist brow, let me in the full ecstacy of superhuman delirium inebriate myself with thy warm breath.

" Beautiful thou art ! thy cheek is rosy, thy head rests upon thy snow-white arm, and the halo of thy fair hair in a gentle disorder surrounds thy forehead.

" Beautiful thou art ! in the quiet rest of thy face I seem to see a ray of paradise, and in the celestial joy which shines in thy looks, I see the image of happy dreams.

" Dream, and in thy sleeping may the rainbow pour its colors, the star their rays, the flowers their perfumes, and may the Holy Virgin* send from her paradise a company of angels to dance around thee."

IV.

There the voice became faint as a sound of a distant sounding harp, and her tired forehead fell on the pillow of the little one. Once again the calm sleep of the old happy days returned to her tired eyes.

The young mother absorbed in that fear which surpasses all fears, from the wicket of the iron door peeped in the dark room, and every movement, every kiss, every noise was a stroke of a poniard which pierced her heart.

---

* The poet is an Italian and a Roman Catholic. Generally in every Italian poems are to be found those addresses to the mother of Jesus.— *The Translator.*

But when all was silent, and there was only heard the cadence of two respirations, softly, softly a keeper crept into the room, advanced silently and without awakening the little one, who was sleeping, took her with him and shut the door.

The mother uttered a cry of joy, which echoed in the wide sonorous vaults, and kissing her dear lost angel with joy, pressed her to her heart, and ran through the dark corridor with her tightly pressed to her motherly arm.

The mad woman awakened at the sound of the strange cry, perceived herself to be alone, looked around, and from the hole in the door, by the light of a dying lamp, she saw the white dress of the fugitive girl. A horrible cry of rage was heard, her eyes were suffused with blood and with a foam on her livid lips she stretched her arms and pushed forward. Three times she shook the invincible door, then fell backward and was a corpse.

XI.

SELIM.

———

TO HIS EXCELLENCY FERDINANDO DE LUCA,

Ambassador of His Majesty the King of Italy.

———

I.

IN ancient times, when Egypt (that land dear to God, cradle of the world's civilization) became the prey of the Mamelukes, and when as yet a wise law had not broken and destroyed the fetters which kept the wretched people slaves to the inconstant humour of their pretty masters ;—who, often at their foolish and wilful fancy, condemned to an awful death or wicked tortures their slaves, guilty of naught save a too great fidelity, or a too blind obedience—in that dreadful age of crimes, when in cold blood the most beautiful maidens were taken by force from their father's roofs to sacrifice their beauties, their celestial candour and every affection, always living hesitating and uncertain of to-morrow, a horrible deed affected the hearts of all, and when narrated often moved the listeners to tears. The patriotic guitar long time seconded the sad songs of the troubadours who repeated to the people the sad history. It was there that I become acquainted with this story, and I will narrate it to thee, kind reader.

Come, then, with me, follow me to the mansion of the great ruler of many large tribes, the absolute monarch of golden lands, of girls willing victims of his lust, and of thousands obedient slaves.

Surrounded by the gentle arms and the electric touch of loose tresses, amidst laughter, caresses and the ascending vortex of the sweet perfumes, the wicked ruler, tired of the work of the day, inebriated whiles away the time, and smiles and enjoys the great favours granted him by God and his prophet.

And yet, amongst these joys, a wicked thought sometimes played over the wrinkled forehead of this tyrant, and often his panting breath give forth a sigh; he flies then, and taking himself away from the embraces, biting his close pressed lips with convulsed rage, like a madman he runs, trampling and destroying everything in his passage. Soon at such a noise with bended looks and hands crossed on his breast, come to him a faithful slave with dreadful face monstrously contracted at the time he suffered the torture which deprived him of his manhood. Iniquitous law, eternal shame of our century! He tries to sooth the scarcely suppressed cries of his master, thus humbly speaking, " Pray be not angry at my presence.

C

A slave do not deserve thy sorrow ; if, fool, she dares to resist thy will, condemn her to the lashes which have made obedient so many other proud ones like her. The whip will satisfy thy wishes better than the merciful kindness with which since six months thou hast treated her. And why carest thou for her so much ? Has not the harem beauties more enchanting than she ?"

"More enchanting, yes—but not so dear to my heart ! All the beauties gathered there and faithful to me cannot purchase a single flash of her smile ! Oh ! if I could only win her heart, all the palaces, all the gems, all the houris, all my treasures, all, I would joyfully give in exchange of this love which torments me. When I think of her beauty, of her virgin purity, of her sweet and gentle looks, of her smile—and that I cannot call her mine ! Oh ! then I wish to condemn her to a thousand atrocious deaths ! But as soon as her heaven-like face confronts my wrath—looking . at her my anger vanishes—and, coward that I am! pity assails me. My thoughts ardently fly to her, and since six months I have felt neither peace nor rest."

"Leave to me, sire, the care of this girl. Trust to the skilfulness of your slave who cares too much for his prince's welfare."

"And what wouldst thou attempt ? "

"Nothing,—or at least very little ! Shortly Agar will be obedient, I promise you to-day and I am not wont to forswear myself."

And presently the monster added so many other reasons, he tried so many and different ways that at last the tyrant charged him with bringing the restive one to his wishes. The old wretch inly felt glad at this order. Vile wretches like him in their impotence being generally cruel, and said to himself, " To us now, fair girl, now I have the tools to cut thy pinions. Disdainful little bird, thou must submit," and thus saying he, through the silent spacious halls, proceeded to seek the unhappy maiden.

II.

" O, my guitar, pour out into the air the complaints which so richly overflow from the saddened heart, and repeat the continual tortures of my soul which resembles a fire that languishes but does not die !

" Sweet companion undivided in the grief thou wast already my companion in those days, in which seated on the border of my river, thus I spoke to Allah, ' Allah ! I only adore three things, my father's grave, my mother and my Selim ! I implore thy prophet that he may keep them, so that finally in complete happiness I should bend before thy throne and with a sincere heart; O, Eternal God, I could address thee a hymn of thanksgiving.'

" But Allah the cruel ! jealous of mortal happiness, in a single day, ravished all from me, while thou, my guitar, so dear companion in my sorrows, always remainest faithful to me. Come on ! let us sing !"

Thus seated on a feathered chair in a spacious gilded hall silent as a tomb, had spoken the unhappy Agar more beautiful than the sun.

She is of Abyssinian descent, by force torn away
from her native place, obliged to offer with fear her in-
genuous smile and her heavenly form to the cruel tyrant
who had bought her. Bright, she has blue eyes, mirrors
of paradise, and lips which often incline to celestial
kisses and hold treasures of white pearls. A veil,
traitor coverlet, wraps all her gentle person, which is
softly extended with the guitar in her hands, turning her
looks to the sky, sighing, trembling, and speaking to herself.

"Mother! O despairing thoughts! What yet awaits
me so afar for ever from thee, my beloved? Vain is hope
for my broken heart. To me nothing is left except death!
O, yes! Sweet is the peace of a tomb this refuge, heaven,
has preserved for the unhappy."

But here she is suddenly surprised by a strange and
light noise; she remained mute with fixed eyes, half open
lips and straining listening ears, but she hears nothing, or
at least she thinks so in the cloister-like silent palace
where she is buried.

Again she let loose the bridle of her thoughts, and carried on the wings of love she flies to the days in which
her young lover, mounted on a noble courser rode away
in quest of great deeds. She longs for his return, and
she perceives her loved one acclaimed; she dreams of his
promise, of the immense joy of an everlasting affection,
and at these happy thoughts she laughs, weeps—and a
hidden blush colours the virgin cheeks and makes her
such a proud model of beauty, that even God would vene-
rate his own immortal work. Again the noise is repeated,

a strange noise resembling the clapping of hands in a certain manner as for a signal. Agar became again motionless, and not long after she heard the distant echo of stirring steps, and finally before she lost her senses there appeared before her a man with his face covered, who immediately fell at her feet in an imploring attitude with joined hands, like one who addresses his prayers to the Holy Virgin. The dark face of the prostrated man, the dress he wears, alas ! too well known to the unhappy, soon led her to believe that he was one of the keepers, and judging him a madman, trembled; nevertheless her heart inspired by love's powerful voice guided her looks to the person before her, and then trembled again first for surprise, for joy, for hope, and then at length for fear. Finally is heard a sharp cry, pronouncing one word, Selim !—and that was all, a river of tears having overwhelmed her voice.

III.

Yes, it was Selim, a warrior born in the Arabian deserts, and while yet young deprived of both parents. A brother of his mother who in Abyssinia had a wealth of flocks, servants, and all that humanity could wish for had taken with him the grief-stricken young orphan who in his friendly tent had found hospitality and new affections. Bright, and fond of hard work, of dangers, he sometimes mounted on a fiery horse without bridle or saddle, was wont to run over the immense surrounding plain, busy with dangerous hunting and with bloody and ungrateful struggles ; or, armed with a lance or glittering sword, he devoted many hours of the day to warlike occupations. Thus while his valiant soul aimed at noblest exploits his frame grew stronger, his hand surer, and his eye keener.

But one day when, later than usual, he was returning to his abode, near to a spring he saw a beautiful, chaste, innocent maiden completely ignorant of the joyful and fatal deceit of love. At the neighing of the horse she suddenly turned her face perceiving the brave Selim, who, proud and beautiful, admirably guided his fierce horse which, knowing how well his master was surely seated in its croup, playfully gave a graceful and nimble leap, as though he would make known the honour of carrying the valiant master who held the bridle.

Both Agar and Selim's souls were suddenly struck by the same feeling. The former lowered her looks to the ground, while her cheeks became red. Selim's heart beats quicker in his breast, and surprised at the appearance of such a beauty remained silent, as immersed in profound contemplation. After awhile dismounting, with slow paces he approached the girl, and with sweet and vibrating voice, asked a sip of the fresh and pure water which shined in the ray of the moon. She soon granted his request, while her uncertain looks wandered timidly now at the ground and now at the young man's face. Selim, mute himself, with covetous and admiring eye followed the enchantress while she moved, furtively glancing to see if anybody followed, her heart telling her the noble youth was

near, and although inly she felt joyful, she did not dare to
turn her head. Arrived near to her house, she departed
hesitatingly with uncertain hands waved a greeting to
her cavalier. He stayed to contemplate her, and his
heart became so full of her, that he passed part of the
night standing in the same spot, where the beautiful
unknown had disappeared.

From that time Agar had no more peace, and the youth
became sad and thoughtful. Always at eventide slowly
he went nursing the hope of seeing her from afar, and if
sometimes provident faith brought her also there, and he
was able to exchange with her only a word, he judged
himself the happiest of mortals, and gave out the joy and
fulness of his soul in gay soliloquies, taking the ground
and breeze as confidants of the hopes of his heart. Agar
on her side poured in the bosom of her pious mother the
story of her love. She carefully listened to her, feeding
with warm words and flattering hopes the flames of a
virgin love. Scarcely had two months elapsed when a
profound and immense grief seized on Selim. Cruel
death ravished him of his uncle and left alone the orphan
who, at this unforeseen and sad event, fell the prey of a
fatal illness. Agar and her mother day and night watched
over the bed of the sick, and the care of these two pitiful
ones benefitted Selim so much, that although near to
the grave, he recovered new life;—such is the power
concealed in love.

From the day of his complete recovery, these two never
more separated, the same roof lodged both, the same air
fed both, and thus they grew beautiful, enjoying the

blessed joy which pure and innocent love pours into the young soul. O ! how often running over the surrounding green meadows, wrapped by the brightness of the moon, they repeated to the mild and embalmed breeze the sweet hopes they cherished. O ! how many promises they exchanged ! They were happy, and to sanctify the chain which binds for ever their hearts was needed only a ring ; when the Egyptian prince prompted by unjust thirst for war, called to arms all those who could carry a sword or a bow, and who knew how to use them. More than thirty thousand answered to his call, and went to defend the prince, who in the meantime searched sweet distractions and shameful pleasures in the midst of tearful slaves sold to his caprices. The cry of war struck the Abyssinian land, and soon to its defence also rose thousands and thousands of swords, grasped by free hands, the freedom of their fatherland, first and more powerful of every affection, piercing their hearts, and gladly those champions fly in defence of the Aybssinian country. Selim was amongst the first to depart, leaving in tears his dear Agar and her mother in the place where they had passed beautiful and happy days. His patriotic love overcame every other feeling, and mounted in his saddle, girded the blessed sword, and pressing Agar to his breast, quick as a flash of lightning he departed for the general place of rendezvous. O ! how the sad Agar wept her love ! How many and how fervid were the prayers she addressed to Almighty God, that He might spare her beloved.

IV.

It is late in the night, everywhere reigns a silence harmonious in its mystery, soothing the soul, and making all the feelings enraptured towards the spheres on high to search in the infinite vault a compensation for our hopes, a feeble ray of the only light, which could guide us to truth. The pale moon, with her cool brightness, inundates the immense plain, and everything with vaporous colours veils the broad horizon of the vast desert. From time to time the monotonous cry of some owl in search of a companion, or the far roar of a hungry, wild and cruel beast troubles only this calm silence. A maiden also defies the night's rigor, a maiden who clothed in white, with nimble feet and palpitating heart turns everywhere her anxious glances, and after listening, stands just as a benighted traveller, tired and lost in a heath, would inquire with searching eyes from which side may come the longed-for help. Her expectation is vain, and the sad one discovering nothing, bending her head in her virgin bosom, weeps, and as drop by drop the tears furrow her beautiful face she opens her lips to a prayer, the greatest comfort of every tormented soul.

"O, Father of the wretched who rulest this universe! O, supreme prophet of a severe law! O, beautiful stars, silvered stars, be illumined by my prayers! You have taken away from me the bright warrior, my only hope, sending him to the dreadful vicissitudes of war, leaving me alone with broken heart, while my mind, incessantly carried on the wings of love, flies to him. Pray, return him back to me. I kneel and beseech thee with all the warmth of my heart."

At this moment of the prayer her voice failed, and she starts up, moved by a secret voice, which whispers harmonious songs. She gazes at the extreme horizon, and it seemed her to see something glitter like a ray, which runs and splinters reflected by the shining blades of warriors.

It seemed to her she heard a stamping, a deep neighing rendered deeper and tremendous by the solitude of the place. She bends herself and places her ear to the ground. The stamping is becoming more distinct,—it comes nearer,—and before she could think of escape, she is surrounded by a large band of horsemen with horrid faces and blazing eyes, loaded with murderous arms.

The poor girl tried to fly, but was unable—too late! They with brutal strength pressed her frame. A piercing cry was the only answer she could give to the leader of the iniquitous band. She saw nothing else, she heard nothing more, having fainted, and when again she opened her eyes, she finds herself lying in a dreadful dark cave, with more than twenty other girls, all like her, brought there by force and infamously wrested from their roofs, victims, alas! of the same cruel fate. Shrieks, blasphemies, horrid laughs, moans, tears, sobs, were the usual sounds repeated by the echoes of those walls. For five days she remained mute, deprived of all sense, feeble and a prey to the strongest delirium; finally on the sixth day she arrived at a large town, changing her life to gilded saloons. There, after many months, Selim saw

her and called down imprecations on destiny. This was
the story Agar narrated him with such an accent of truth
and pain as to lacerate Selim's heart.

V.

"Hush! for pity, Agar! hush! do not go on! Thou
then dost not perceive my grief and the devilish rage
which rises in me, at the abject situation in which I find
thee?

"Truce to sorrow and useless tears! These are unworthy of a man! Not vainly has God allowed me to remain
safe in the fatal struggle in which so many of our stronger
and greater than I left their lives; not in vain, He has
brought me to these unfriendly places, only that I may
appease my wrath in useless tears. No, I must take thee
away from hence and immediately—"

"What darest thou?"

"What love dictates, and duty commands. God has
been pleased to keep thee yet pure, but thou must not
defy longer the will and the anger of the cruel sire
Trust me, think, O dearest, that I am near to thee and
ready to watch and protect thee. I only need a guide,
and be ready at the first signal."

"Selim, think of thyself, of my mother, who languishes
alone, unhappy, and ignorant of our destiny. Do not put
thyself to the hazard of an unwise undertaking."

"I had hoped thou wouldst have spoken in a very
different way! How? Is then this the answer to the

deep love I feel for thee ?   Be whatever the risk of my enterprise I must try it.   Listen to me and endeavor to help me.   When darkness comes, when the prince will sit at the table, swift I will creep here, and will open the garden's secret door which leads to Nile.   There, unseen in a coach, I will await Achmet, a faithful friend who has introduced me here, wrapped in this deccitful suit in which thou seest me.   He will take care of all.   Soon as he will arrive, disrobe thyself of thy garments, and taking a male attire, which he cautiously will bring thee, hasten to the garden door where I will be waiting."

" The scheme is bold, and great is the risk ; art thou sure of Achmet ? "

" As of myself.   He has been with me since the day when at Kartoum I saved him from death.   He owes me his life and I well know his fidelity.   He has accompanied me in my search for thee, and to this faithful friend I owe the joy of having seen thee again.   Be then ready, and at ease, trust to me, beloved girl, and hope ! "

" Selim ! Selim ! with these words thou fillest my heart with measureless joy.   Will I then see again my fatherland and my mother—poor unhappy woman ?   Can I dry the tears which flow from her eyes ?   Could I be free again, and with thee ?   O, I faint !"

" No, subdue thy feelings.   For a few instants more let thy lips be mute as the tomb, and let thy eye be closed as a blind.   Trust to me and Allah !   Come to my breast and embrace me, in this last embrace......"

" And last it will be !" was suddenly thundered by a horrid voice ; and at the door appeared the Egyptian prince, fearful in his looks, a whip in his hand, the sword hanging at his left side, with swollen eyes inflamed with wrath, and followed by the cruel chief of his vile slaves, faithful keeper of the harem.

A hoarse cry came out from Selim's heart, while Agar without knowledge fell to the ground.

Two days after, in a dark cell of the large princely harem, stretched on the floor, everywhere surrounded by blood, which like a stream flowed from her body, near to death lay Agar, the beautiful girl of sixteen years whose tender flesh the whip had torn, while the cruel tyrant looks at the bloody limbs; bloody, yes, but still beautiful, and hugs himself and laughs at the martyrdom of the unhappy girl.

"Thou," he tells her, "hast despised me as a friend and as a lover, fear now my justice, which has condemned thee to die."

Amongst the most atrocious sufferings, forsaken Agar breathed her last breath in the horrid prison, her convulsing lips opening to pronounce a name,—the name of her dear Selim. Her virgin soul, like a rose broken on the stem scarcely open to life and warmth, ascended to the feet of her creator.

History says nothing about Selim, only one day a fisherman who sad was returning from his unfruitful fishing, found on the bosom of the Nile the body of a young man. Everyone noticed the proud and beautiful face though cold and thin. Popular voice says this was the body of the brave Selim—victim of the jealous tyrant. By the same fisherman who found it, the body was buried

in a solitary shady place, amongst beautiful flowers tend-
ed by pious hands.

Often a tired traveller bound homeward would bend
himself there, and there, too, go a sad poet, who thinking
over the fate of the buried one, in verses burning with
noble wrath imprecates the cruel prince and the barbarous
destiny of that unfortunate country.

XII.

POLAND.

1883.

TO COL. C. S. GZOWSKI.

Fur alles Heilige entbraunt.

KÖRNER.

THEY come! They are here! Welcome Poles! Let us beat off the dust from their swollen feet,—let us cover with dainty dishes the hospitable table! Free citizens, let us take in our hands the cups! Never similar fugitives have reached our shores. Never driven by storms guests more celebrated than these warriors in mourning have landed as suppliants on our soil.

A despot, elated by his power, had said: Poland must die! To wash away the insult I have received, I will grind her forehead under my horse's hoof; I will cause future generations to cry out on account of my revenge! I will crush this people as a reed is crushed by a granite block! I will make them feel the weight of my hand,

and to-morrow, without seeing a vestige of them, one may go through those rebel cities.

To-morrow! He thought so, and the self-conceited, during ten months, without gaining any advantage, pushed on armies, which one after another he saw instantly destroyed,—melted in a ground sparkling with fire.— The reed became an oak, whose unbended branches the invisible root, under the thickened blood, resisted long, and seemed to receive strength with the buffet of the hurricane.

Hurrah!....Like a whirlwind o'er the wild steppes, barbarous without a name, run in full gallop, uttering loud and discordant cries, and at the same moment in which they thought to fall upon the spoils they stumbled on corpses. Hurrah! Hurrah! Ere long these warriors without renown, appearing in a day of battle, were broken, as wave falls on wave already broken on the sand.

O! how grand to see the Polish soldiers, at the sound of the clarion, rush to the contest, and set at defiance the far discharges of the guns, charging the squadrons, in front of the squares. O! how grand to see dauntless battalions marching to the attack, and soon as a battery had thundered on them, carry the redoubt, and extinguish the murderous fire. But, O vileness! A chief of sad memory, who might have ended his life in freedom, keeping untarnished his honor, opened his traitor hand to the oppressor's gifts, and Poland expiring, overpowered amidst blood and cries, fell down under the murderers, as a wounded soldier, fallen on his knee, dies inflicting a last blow,—and the conqueror trod upon her trampled bosom. Poland, where are now thy sons? Happy those who died,—sacrificed in honor of the God worshipped by Russia! They need no tears. Others—O, folly!—without shame, without remorse, are dragged in the desert, dying by slow degrees of hunger and misery. Others, wandering through the world, addressing to cold sympathizers frozen by their own interests, are eating a bitter crust reluctantly given.

Nevertheless, thou yet livest, sublime Poland! Though persecuted, courage remains. Leave time, to do his duty. The cut tree after years has grown again, and in the freedom of the air again exalts a higher top. Often the wounded bear has risen again against the hunter, killing him. Often the cold ashes have secretly hidden the first spark of a great conflagration.

It is God who sends them to us. To those sacred guests let us offer with pride a happy retreat. Shame to us if a hair only falls from their heads! Everywhere their steps are full of insults. Every one to flatter the tiger, wishes to deliver his victim. How noble! how gallant!

And we, what are we to do? Defend these valiant ones who have come with branches in their hands, and share with them our homes—our bread; shielding them with our bodies against all those slaves who would have become pale in the day of battle; and to better maintain our oath, bite, if necessary, our last cartridge.

Or if you, our leaders who feasted the powerful, judge that these are sentiments too noble, add a new shame to

D

the past ones, and, like Iscariot, receive the price of blood. You will be welcomed at the court, you will receive insignia worthy of your hearts, as it needed great strength to defy an insult, and contempt is always a heavy weight on one's very forehead.

But then we shall be the last men! But when in foreign lands we shall be asked which is our own country, we shall blush and own with shame who we are!— But we cannot bluster more, without being treated as cowards, worthy of blows.

Woe to him who will refuse the exile his help. Perhaps—who knows?—from our enslaved Switzerland, we may some day have to fly in search of a place where to hide our life; and perhaps, we, too, may be in search of help,—escaped from the executioner of an implacable master, perhaps one day moaning we will tend our arms to alms, and then we will reap the seed we have sown.

Soldiers! my companions! I appeal to your souls!— You will not suffer that oppressed men cannot hope to find peace under your flag. Our honor is our own,—nobody will dare to chase these unhappy ones in our name, to make us infamous. Ah! if we shall be obliged with shame to lower our eyes, instead of proudly upholding our despised flag! Rather let us with our own hands drag it in the dust!

They come! They are here! Welcome, Poles! Let us beat off the dust from their swollen feet; Let us cover with dainty dishes the hospitable table. Free citizens, let us take in our own hands the cups! Never similar fugitives have reached our shores.   Never driven by the storms guests more celebrated than these warriors in mourning, as suppliants, have landed on our soil.

XIII.

FOR THE POOR.

———

TO THE HON. ALEXANDER MORRIS, P. C.,

Late Lieut.-Governor of Manitoba and the North West Territory.

———

"He who giveth to the poor, lendeth to the Lord."

YE wealthy and happy of this world, when in your winter feasts the flying dance inundates you with its sprightliness,—when you see shine and sparkle all around you crystals, mirrors, burning chandeliers, circles of light, and gladness on the face of your guests,— while a golden bell ringing in your apartments changes to joyful notes the grave sounds of the hours,—tell me, have you never thought that devoured by famine, some poor wretch, shivering in the dark, observes your dancing shadows across the windows of your gilded saloons?

Have you never thought that there, exposed to the frost and snow, is a father without work tortured by hunger? Hear how he mutters in a subdued voice: "How

many blessings for a single person ! How many friends
enjoys themselves at his banquet ! How happy is this rich
man ! his children smile at him, with the price of their
toys how much bread might be bought for mine !" And
then to your feasts he compares in his mind, his squalid
hearth, never brightened by the flame—his famishing
children, their mother's rags,—their grand-mother stretched on the straw—who, through the winter, alas ! is
already cold enough for the grave.

God has established these gradations of human fortune.
Few are invited to the banquet of happiness, and all are
not seated equally at their ease. A law which here seems
unjust and bad says to the one "Enjoy," to the other
"Envy." This thought is sombre, bitter, inexorable, and
ferments silently in the hearts of the miserable. O ! ye
rich, ye happy of the day, lulled to sleep by pleasure, let
it not be they who tear from your hands those super-
fluous goods which they regard with envy. O let it be
charity.

That ardent charity, which the poor idolize—mother
of those to whom fortune is a step-mother, which raises
and sustains those who are trampled on, and who in the
hour of need sacrificing herself like the martyr God of
whom she follows the footsteps will say, "This is my
bread, this is my blood." Let it be she, ye rich, let it be
she who to nourish the indigent and to save your souls,
shall tear with unsparing hand from the arms of your
daughters—from the breasts of your wives—jewels, dia-
monds. ribbons, laces, pearls, sapphires—jewels always
false—jewels always vain.

Give, ye rich. Charity is the sister of prayer. Alas!
If some old man, stiffened by the icy cold, vainly kneels
at your marble threshold,—if the little children, with
their red half-frozen hands seize on the crumbs left by
your revels, surely the face of the Lord will be turned
away from you. Give, that God, who endows families,
may give strength to your sons and grace to your daughters,—that your vine may always produce sweet fruits,—
that the ripe corn may overflow your granaries,—that
you may become better, and that in your dreams you
may see the angels visit you.

Give, for the day must come when earth leaves you.
Your alms will form for you a treasure on high. Give,
that it may be said "He pitied us!"—that the indigent
whom the tempests freeze,—that the poor who suffer in
the midst of your feasts,—may regard with a less jealous
eye the threshold of your palaces. Give, that you may
be beloved by the God who made himself a man,—that
your dwelling may be calm and fraternal. Give, that
some day, at your last hour, for all your sins, you may
have in Heaven the prevailing prayer of the beggar.

XIV.

THE NIGHT OF OCTOBER.

TO MY BROTHER, CAVALIER GIOVANNI SORVILLO.

POET.

THE pain I suffered has vanished like a dream, and the faint remembrance it has left I can only compare to those mists which rise with the dawn and disperse in the dew.

MUSE.

What ailed thee, my poet, and what was the pain that parted thee from me? Alas! I yet feel its sad effects. What is this unknown grief I have so long bewailed?

POET.

It was a vulgar pain well known to men, but when our heart is grieved, we always believe, poor fools that we are, that nobody before us has known sorrow.

MUSE.

Only the sorrow of a vulgar mind can be called vulgar.
Friend, reveal this sad misery of thy heart; believe me;
speak with confidence. The severe God of silence is one
of the brethren of death; complaint brings consolation,
and often a single word has spared remorse.

POET.

If I were to speak of my pain, truly I should not know
by what name to call it,—if it be love, folly, pride, experience, or if it could be of profit to anybody—but as we
are now alone, seated by the fire, I will tell my story.
Take thy lyre, and let my memory awaken softly at the
sound of thy notes.

MUSE.

Before you relate your sorrows, Poet, are you cured?
Think, that to-day you must speak without love or hatred;
recollect I have received the sweet name of a consoler,
and do not make me the accomplice of the passions that
have ruined thee.

POET.

I am so well cured of my malady, that sometimes I
doubt if it ever existed; and where I risked my existence, instead of myself, I fancy I see the face of a stranger. Muse, be without fear, we may both without danger

confide in the voice of thy inspiration. It is sweet **to** weep, it is sweet to smile, at the remembrance of ills **we** might have forgotten.

MUSE.

Like a watchful mother at the cradle of a beloved child, I trembling turn to thy heart which was closed to me. Speak, friend, my attentive lyre already follows the accents of thy voice, and in a ray of light, like a beautiful vision, pass by the shades of other days.

POET.

Days of work, the only days in which I really lived. O, solitude, thrice beloved! God be praised, at last I have returned to my old study! Poor room, walls so often deserted, dusty chairs, faithful lamp! O, my palace, my little world, and thou young immortal Muse, God be praised, we are going again to sing! Yes, I will open my soul, you shall know all, and I will relate you the ills that a woman can do,—for a woman it was, my poor friend, (alas, perhaps you already know it,) a woman to whom I submitted as a serf submits to his master. Detested yoke, it was there my heart lost its force and its youth, and yet near my mistress I had fancied I should find happiness. When in the evening near the brook we walked together on the silvery sand, when the white spectre of the poplar showed us the road from afar, I can yet see by the rays of the moon, her beautiful frame leaning on my arm. Let us speak no more of it. I did not foresee where fortune would lead me; doubtless the anger of the Gods had need of a victim, for my attempt to be happy has been punished as a crime.

MUSE.

The image of a sweet remembrance has just presented itself to thy thoughts. Why fearest thou to retrace its track ? Young man if fortune has ·been cruel, do like her, smile on thy first love.

POET.

No, it is at my misfortune that I have acquired a right to smile at. Muse, I said I would without passion relate my sorrows, my dreams, my madness, and that I would tell thee the time, the hour and the occasion. It was, I recollect, a night of autumn, sad and cold, like to-night; the murmur of the wind with monotonous noise nursed dark cares in my troubled mind. I was at the window, expecting my mistress, and listening in the obscurity, I felt such a distress in my heart, that I conceived the suspicion of an infidelity. The street where I lodged was dark and deserted; some shadows passed, a lantern in their hands. When the wind whistled in the half-closed door one heard in the distance what seemed a human sigh. I know not—to say the truth—to what sad presentiment my inquiet spirit then abandoned itself. I recalled in vain the remains of my courage, and I felt a tremble when I heard the clock strike. She came not. Alone with down-cast eyes I looked anxiously at the walls and the road ; and I have not told thee what a senseless ardour that inconstant woman lighted in my bosom. Her alone I loved in the world, and to live a day without her seemed to me a destiny more dreadfnl than death ; still I remember in that fearful night I made a long effort to break my chain. A hundred times I called her perfidious and false. I reminded myself of all the ills she had caused me. Alas ! at the recollection of her fatal beauty what ills, what griefs were still unappeased ? At length the day broke. Tired with vain expectation I fell into slumber on the rails of the balcony. I opened my eyes at the rising dawn and let my dazzled eyes wander around me. Suddenly at a turning of a narrow lane I heard on the gravel stealthy footsteps. It is she. She enters. Whence comest thou ? Last night what hast thou done ? answer, what would'st thou ? Who brings thee at this hour ?............Whilst I alone on this balcony watch and weep, in what place, to whom did'st thou smile ? Perfidious, audacious woman, is it possible you come to me ? What askest thou ? By what horrible thirst darest thou seek to draw me to thy exhausted arms ? Go, retire spectre of my beloved—return to the grave if you are risen from it—leave me to forget forever the joy of my youth, and when I think of thee to believe that I have dreamed.

MUSE.

Calm thyself; I conjure thee. Thy words make me

shudder ; thy wound is near to re-open. Alas ! it is very deep, and the miseries of this world are so long ere they are effaced. Forget my child, and from thy heart drive the name of that woman I will not pronounce.

POET.

Shame to thee who first taught me treachery, and maddened me with horror and rage. Shame to thee woman of the dark eye, whose fatal love buried in the shade my spring and my bright days. Thy voice, thy smiles, thy corrupting glances taught me to curse even the appearance of happiness ; thy youth, thy charms reduced me to despair, and if I no longer believe in tears it is because I have seen thee weep. Shame to thee ! I was as simple as a child ; like a flower at the dawn my heart opened to thy love—sure that heart without defence could easily be abused—but to leave it its innocence was still easier. Shame to thee ; thou was't the mother of my first sorrows, and thou causest a fountain of tears to flow from my eyes —still it flows and nothing will ever cure—but in that bitter source at least I will bathe, and I shall forget, I hope, thy abhorred remembrance.

MUSE.

Poet ; it is enough. Though the illusions with the faithless one lasted but a day, do not curse that day when thou speakest of her—if thou desirest to be loved respect thy love—if the effort is too great for human weakness to pardon the ills that come to us from others, spare thyself at least the torments of hatred, and in default of pardon let oblivion come. The dead sleep in peace in the bosom of the earth ; and thus should sleep the feelings which are extinguished ; the relics of the heart have also their ashes. Do not let our hands touch these sacred remains. Why, in this narration of a vivid suffering, will you only see a dream and a deluded love ? Does Providence act without a motive ? or, thinkest thou the God who struck thee struck inadvertently ? The blow of which thou complainest has perhaps saved thee, child, by that thy heart was opened. Man is an apprentice, and sorrow is his master, and no one knows himself until he has suffered. Hard is the law, but supreme, old as the world and the fate, that we must receive the baptism of misfortune, and at such sad price everything must be bought. The crops to ripen have need of dew. The symbol of joy is a broken plant wet with rain and covered with flowers. Did'st thou not say thou wert cured of thy folly ? Art thou not young, fortunate, well received by all—and those light pleasures which make life desirable—what would'st thou care for them if thou had'st not wept ? When on the decline of day seated in the earth thou drinkest at liberty, say, would'st thou raise thy glass so heartily if thou had'st not paid the price of thy gaiety ? Would'st thou love flowers, meadows, the green shade, the sonnets of Petrarch, and the song of the birds, Michel Angelo and the arts, Shakespeare and nature, if thou didst not find some of these old sighs in them ? Wouldst thou understand the ineffable harmony of the heavens, the silence of the night, the murmur of the waves, if in some other places fever and sleeplessness had not made thee think of eternal rest ?— Hast thou not now a fair mistress—and when in going to sleep thou pressest her hand, the distant recollection of thy youth does not render her divine smiles more sweet ? Do you not walk together in the midst of flowering woods, on the silvery sand, and in that palace of verdure ? Does the white spectre of the poplar no longer show thee the road by the ray of the moon ? Do'st thou not see as then by the rays of the moon a beautiful frame lean her hand on thy arm—and if in thy path thou shouldst meet with fortune, would'st thou not follow her gaily singing ? Of what then do'st thou complain ? Immortal hope is revived in thee by the hand of misfortune. Oh, my child, pity her the unfaithful who formerly made the tears flow from thy eyes. Wherefore would'st thou hate the experience of thy youth, and detest an ill which has rendered thee better. Pity her—she is a woman—and God made thee, when with her, guess by suffering the secret of happiness. Her task was painful. She perhaps loved thee, but destiny willed that she should break thy heart; she knew life, and she made thee know it. Another has culled the fruit of thy sorrow— pity her—her sad love has passed like a dream ; she saw thy wound, but could not close it. Her tears, believe me, were not all deceitful, and even though they were, pity her. Thou now knowest how to love.

POET.

You speak truth. Hatred is impious, it is a shudder-

ing full of horror—when that viper curled up in our heart
unfolds herself. Hear me then, Goddess, and be witness
of my oath. By the blue eyes of my mistress—by the
azure of the firmament—by that brilliant star which
bears the name of Venus, and like a diamond shines from
afar on the horizon—by the kindness of the Creator—by
the tranquil and pure light of the star dear to the travel-
er—by the herbs of the prairie—by the forests—by the
green meadows—by the powers of life—by the productive
force of the universe, I banish you from my memory, remains of an insensate love ; mysterious and dark history
which will sleep with the past—and thou who formerly
hast borne the fame and the sweet name of my beloved,
the instant that I forget thee forever ought also to be the
moment of forgiveness. Let us pardon one another. I
break the chain which united us before God. With my
last tear receive an eternal adieu ; and now, fair dreamer,
now, Muse, to our own loves—sing me some joyous song
as in the first time of our bright days. Already the
fragrant lawn feels the approach of the morning. Come
to walk my dearest, and to smell the flowers of the
garden ; come to see immortal nature rise from the veil
of sleep ; we shall revive with her, at the first ray of
the sun.

XV.

PHANTOMS.

TO WM. OLDRIGHT, ESQ., M.A., M.D.

I.

HOW many beautiful maidens have I seen die! It is destiny? A prey is necessary to death. As the grass must fall under the scythe, so in the ball the quadrille must trample rosy youth under its steps. The fountain by irrigating the valleys must diminish its waters. The lightning must shine but only for a moment. Envious April with its frosts must blight the apple-tree too proud of its odoriferous flowers white as the snow of spring. Yes; such is life. The darkness of night follows the daylight and to all will come the eternal awaking in heaven or the abyss. A covetous crowd sits at the great banquet, but many of the guests leave their places empty and depart before the end.

II.

How many I have seen die! One was fair and blooming. Another seemed to hear celestial music. Another with her arms upholds her bended head—and as the bird which in taking flight breaks the branch on which he rests—her soul had broken her body.

One pale, lost, oppressed by sad delirium pronounced in a low voice a name forgotten by all, another dies away as a sound of a lyre, and another expiring has on her lips the sweet smile of a young angel returning to heaven. All frail flowers—dead as soon as born—halcyons drowned with their floating nests; doves sent from heaven to earth, who, crowned with grace, youth and love numbered their years by the springs.

Dead! What? Already lying under the cold stone! So many charming beings deprived of voice and life! So many lights extinguished! So many flowers faded away! O, let me trample the dried leaves and lose myself in the depth of the woods.

Lovely phantoms! It is there in the woods, when in the dark I am thinking; it is there that by turns they come to listen and to speak to me. The twilight at the same time shows and veils their number, but across the branches and leaves I perceive their glittering eyes.

My soul is a true sister to those beautiful shadows. For me and for them life and death have no laws—sometimes I help their steps—sometimes I take their wings.

F

Ineffable vision in which I am dead as they—they alive
as me. They lend their forms to my thoughts, I see ; O,
yes, I see them. They beckon me to come, and then
hand in hand they dance around a grave, and by degrees
disappearing softly, draw away, and then I think and I
remember.

III.

One specially—an angel—a young Spanish girl! White
hands—her breast swelled by innocent sighs. Black
eyes in which shone the looks of a Creole ; and that in-
definite charm that fresh halo which generally crowns a
head of fifteen.

She died not for love. No ; love had not yet brought
her joy or sorrow ; nothing yet had made her rebel heart
beat, and when everyone in looking at her could not re-
press the words, "How beautiful she is!" none had
yet uttered secretly the word of love. Poor girl ! She
loved dancing too much—it was that which killed her.
The charming ball ! The ball full of delight ! Her ashes
still tremble with a gentle movement—if by chance in a
fair night a white cloud dances round the crescent of the
sky.

She loved dancing too much ! At the approach of a
festival—three days before she was continually thinking
and dreaming of it—and for three nights ladies, music,
dancers never tired troubled her mind in her sleep, and
laughed, and shouted at her pillows.

Jewels, necklaces, silk girdles of waving reflections,

sues lighter than the bee's wings, festoons of ribbons in full baskets, and flowers to buy a palace; all those things occupy her fancy.

Once the festival begun—full of gladness she comes with her joyful sisters, furling and unfurling the fan in her fingers—then sits amongst the silk dresses, and her heart bursts into glad strains with the many-voiced orchestra. What a true delight was it to look at her when she was dancing. Her garment tossed its blue spangles ; her great dark eyes sparkled under the black mantle like a pair of stars under a dark cloud. She was all dance and laughter and mad joy. Child !

We admire her in our sad leisure moments—sad, because never at the ball our hearts were open—and in these balls, as the dust flies on the silk dress, weariness is mixed with pleasure. She, instead—carried by the waltzes or the polkas—was going up and down, hardly breathing—exciting herself with the' sound of the renowned flute—with the flowers ; with the golden candlesticks ; with the attractive feast; with the music of the voices ; with the noise of the steps.

What happiness for her to move, lost in the crowd—to feel her own senses multiply in the dance so as not to be able to know if she was being conveyed by a cloud, or flying leaving the heart, or treading upon a waving sea.

At the approach of the dawn she was obliged to depart and to wait on the threshold till the silken mantle was thrown over her shoulders. Only then this innocent dancer, chilling, felt the morning breeze pass over her bare neck.

Sad morrows those following a ball ! Farewell, dresses and dances, and child-like laughter. In her the obstinate cough succeeds the songs; the fever, with its hectic color, follows the rosy and lively delights, and the bright eyes are changed into lack lustre eyes.

IV.

She is dead ! Fifteen years old—beautiful, happy, adored ! Dead coming out from a ball which immersed all of us in mourning—dead, alas ! And Death with chilly hands wrested her yet dressed from the arms of a mother, mad with anguish, to lay her to sleep in the grave.

To dance at other balls she was ready; Death was in haste to take possession of such a beautiful body, and the same ephemeral roses which had crowned her head and which blossomed yesterday at a feast faded in a tomb.

V.

The unhappy mother, ignorant of her fate, had placed so deep a love on this frail stalk; to have watched her suffering babyhood so long, and to have wasted so many nights in lulling her when she cried—a tiny baby in her cradle. To what purpose ? Now the girl sleeps under the coffin lid, and if in the grave where we have left her some beautiful winter's night a festival of the death should awake her cold corpse, a ghost with dreadful smile, instead of the mother, will preside at her silent toilette,

and will tell her—"Now is the time," and with a kiss
freezing her blue lips, will pass through her hair the
knotted fingers of its skeleton hand, and will lead her
trembling to the ethereal chorus, flitting in darkness, and
at the same time on the grey horizon the moon will shine
pale and full, and the rainbow of the night will colour
with an opal reflection the silvered cloud.

VI.

Young maidens who are invited by the gay ball, with
its seductive pleasures, think of this Spanish girl. She
was gay, and with a merry hand, was gathering the roses
of life, pleasure, youth and love! Poor girl! Hurried
from feast to feast she was sorting the colors of this beautiful nosegay. How soon all vanished! Like Ophelia
carried away by the river, she died gathering flowers.

XVI.

ON THE DEATH OF A GIRL.

TO MY BELOVED MOTHER, FORTUNATA SORVILLO,

Widow Nobile, (neé Nansô).

TWELVE springs had embellished her youth. Poor girl! she could have lived longer ; to her eyes the future was opening full of delight, and her beautiful smile was pure as a golden ray of the sun.

The life of this beloved was the support of her mother's soul. Innocence supports, while virtue defends. She was used to say, " This angel one day will become a woman," and this child was the incarnation of her happiness.

And thou hast lived twelve years embellishing all on thy passage, for twelve years thy mother found her bliss in the looks of thy charming eyes ; for twelve years she had in her soul a continual happiness knowing that thou wast living.

On the waves of life this girl was a calm, and in sorrows was a ray of dawn, and thou, alas! suddenly left us, leaving in our heart an everlasting sadness. Her soul was the human embodiment of the virtues.—the virtues, flowers of heaver, and perfumes of the elect. Afterward a child was needed in the bands of the angels, God singled her out, Death came, and she was no more.

The mother thoughtful, dishevelled, stayed there to look at the body mute for ever. Alas! for a moment it seemed that her life had disappeared with the poor girl for whom the funeral bell was tolling. O! I seem still to see this girl with her rigid, silent frame, and her pale face! O! I see her cold and beautiful, lying on the bed as if she was sleeping in an angelic dream.

I see the lights around her shed their reddish lustre in the humble and sad room. I see yet the friendly hand faithful to its duty, raise up and place her corpse in the coffin. O! when this little body was brought to the churchyard, the mother groaned for her lost happiness. One would have said that her heart wished to follow the coffin, so many were the sobs which poured from her oppressed breast. The day was over, and gave place to another,—and yet the mother has always in her heart her daughter, and seems always to see her angel prostrated by death. Vainly she is invited to many joyful feasts —vain it is to persuade her of the necessity of forgetting, —vainly it is said that life has the same law for all, and that by death hearts are united with God.

Vainly it is repeated to her that the flowers live only a season; that the beautiful dawn which awakes the morning cannot continue; that the children's souls up in heaven live again,—and at our own death they show themselves to us.

The poor mother remains deaf to all these words. Uselessly every one tells her that her daughter is an angel,—that Death must extend its law over all,—that life is an exile in this world,—that all must change. Alas! her heart is broken,—her faith is extinguished The mother cannot believe and will not believe that she is dead; and continually with her tears, asks for her daughter. She requires this girl, who still lives in her mind, with her songs, with her games, and with her gay smile. Sometimes her mind wanders for a moment, and it seems that her soul has risen to the clouds to see if her time had arrived to depart far away from the noise.— Thus she lives amidst our human shadows, always faithful to her daughter,—her dearest love. Many weeks I have heard her cry, and since, I have been told, that she is still weeping.

XVII.

TO THE AUGUST MEMORY

OF HIS MAJESTY

VICTOR EMMANUEL,*

First King of Italy.

TO E. BENDELARI, ESQ.,‡
Vice Consul of Italy in Toronto.

THE dawn scarcely is reddening the sky, and the pleasant enamelled fields of Novara fill the air with such a shower of perfume as to soothe and inebriate all the senses. Every where nature smiles beautiful and

---

* In the presence of God, I swear to observe with loyalty the Constitution ; not to exercise the Royal Authority except according to the laws and in conformity to the same ; to give everybody according to their rights full and exact justice, and to behave in every thing only with a view to the interest, welfare and honor of the nation.—*Oath pronounced by King Victor Emmanuel the 29th March, 1849.*

‡ SIR,—As a representative of our dear country I have taken the liberty of putting your name at the head of this translation.

Accept it from,

Your obedient,

A. A. NOBILE.

flowering, kissed and caressed by the breeze. Nothing seems to trouble the great quietness that there overflows. From time to time only is heard a deep sound, which ever comes nearer and nearer, increasing in such a manner as to seem a thunder concealed amidst the clouds.— At the farther opposite horizon one could hear a similar noise, which also comes near,—and although not a cloud encumbers or tarnishes the blue sky, the roar does not cease, but becomes stronger.

What may be all this immense mass that thou seest moving at thy right? It resembles a big writhing snake, which thus over a rough and long way, drags along the twisted links of its cold body.

On the left the terrified eye sees a like crowd, and afterward. little by little, the short space which divides those living waves quickly disappears.

On the left flashes a lightning to which follows a thunder,—another lightning flashes and a thunder answers on the right,—then a second,—another,—and finally the shouts arise tremendous. At the same time the sky rapidly changes its color, and under a dark cloud of sulphurous dust, envelops both field and contestants. God! Why such a great bloodshed? Shortly, then, O florid plains of Novara, the clod trampled by thousands upon thousands will be bedewed by streams of blood, and morsels of human flesh will cover the splendid emerald of thy coverlet!

But from the left arises a cry of agony, and from the right answer shrieks of death,—already murderous blades shine in the air.

"*Savoy!*" is the cry,—"*Rade.¯ky!*" is the answer; already the raging waves of men rush against each other, —like a foaming tempestuous sea striking tho gentle shore.

On one side the proud tri-color,—on the other the double-pinioned and royal bird; on the left the hope of a better dawn, the love of native country, and free faith,— on the other side the right of the stronger, who hopes to punish the proud folly of Ausonia. Farther a valiant monarch, who obedient to the wish of a faithful people arose to the battle; a prince, scion of an adored ancestry, admired by all ages for its exploits, master of a small but beautiful province, the beloved of his subjects and the model of loyalty. At his side, proudly mounted on a noble courser, nourished at the breast of the Goddess of Freedom, with refulgent eye, is a young Deity, who, searching in the face of his royal parent, hardly bridles the ardor by which he is urged to fight this sacred battle which for Italy is a last trial for redemption.

The battle grows always more and more terrible, the impatient horses print their hoofs upon the fallen, and continually is heard the noise of the fulminating thundering canons. It is impossible that Heaven can any more favour this dreadful carnage. The tricolor flag of Italy is lowered. The terrible Lombards fly, and the Savoyards cannot fight.

The white uniformed victorious Austrians trample upon the bent Ausonian heads. Awful sight! The flowery ground is all hidden by corpses. Piedmont, cover thyself;

thy hope is extinguished; thy resuscitated faith already become a dream.

Struck by this most cruel fate, Charles Albert perceiving himself alone, uncertain of the future, looking at the numerous soldiers who had fallen on the field in his behalf, cursing his horrible perverse destiny, thus speaks to the son who at his side, dropping noble sweat, was awaiting the orders of his princely father. "Heaven's wrath descends on me, my son. Vain it is to struggle still; all abandon me, I hope no more; and again I see hard destiny for Italy.

"For what, then. all these fights, those dead, and this grief, if again the Ausonian land has to return into slavery?

"The power of this crown is vain, its weight already oppresses me, I cannot withstand the pain; take it, thou, my son, fortune perhaps will smile more propitious on thy valour!

"Put this crown on thy head, and try to wrest the broken heritage from cruel servitude. Thou wilt gain what thy old father has lost. Thou wilt return to fight anew.

"Keep thyself faithful to the people's rights, this being a holy decree written in heaven. Victor, on this bloody field I surrender thee the frail throne's dreadful power." *

---

* The circumstances under which I take the reins of the government, are such, that without the most efficient help of all hardly could I accomplish my unique wish, the good of the country. Now your purpose must be to maintain safe and unhurt the honour, to consolidate our constitutional institutions, I am ready to make a solemn oath.—*Proclamation of King Victor Emmanuel, on the 27th March 1849.*

Since this horrible day had passed two lustrums! Two lustrums of hidden struggles and horror!—of tears,—of griefs; two lustrums of indelible honour to Ausonia.

But all the tears poured, all the pain suffered were incense offered on God's altar, were in the sight of heaven an accepted pledge that Italy shall rise again radiant of faith.

And the same young prince educated to misfortunes, who once ascended on a tottering throne, now commands an army guiding it to glory, and fulfilling in this way his sacred oath.

The avenging and beautiful victorious flag of the three beloved colours is already unfolded in the air, severe avenger of shame and holy grief.

From the frosty Alps to the smoking Vesuvius, from Scylla' to Gortz, already with joy all Italy awakens panting, and each right hand brandishes the redeemer blade.

And joined in a fraternal chain with the French these two descend to fight from the Alps, and shortly we shall see the flowery and charming valley of the Mincio become red with blood.

O great day of Palestro, O sun who wast shining on that day, thou well hast enlightened all the exploits of those valiant avengers of dear Italy, the beautiful country where the *si* is spoken.

Only a mind higher than mine could paint the valorous deeds done in this glorious day. Can a mortal narrate a divine work ? And divine it was,—and history always will call divine St. Martin and Palestro !

*   *   *

Sadly, sadly the bell gives a trembling sound, and far off announces to the faithful believing people a wicked event sadder than death.

The city, the ancient old seat of the humble fisherman, Rome, mother of the faith, of the supreme and threefold love ; Rome, once august and now papal, nest of temporal power ; Rome at last if surrounded by the valiant men who before had fought for unity.

Vain are your bonds which Victor will break as once of yore did the austere founder of the Greek empire. But the bronze avenger is thundering, the friendly army is coming. Italy ! Italy ! Let the joy of the unhappy say how eagerly the people in that day awaited thee.

Victor ! Thou who hast opened thy royal heart at the cry which thou hast heard* arise from one shore to the other, come now to conquer, everyone awaits thee.

Descend brave deliverer king, and brandish the same refulgent sword which once, as thou rememberest, thou hadst unsheathed in defence of thine own and thy ancestor's throne.

And he already listened the unanimous voice of his

---

* Words pronounced by Victor Emmanuel in his speech to the Parliament on the 10th January, 1859.

sons, comes—sees—hastens to conquer at Porta Pia! Let history in its records take note of such valour.

The Savoyard prince, faithful to his word, in his noble breast had nourished a hope, the most holy hope of redeeming the country which so long had remained in slavery and mourning.

The breach is open, swift rushes on the narrow path the Italian soldier; and quickly raising the proud flag, casts his eyes on the great city.

Victory! Victory! the old streets resound with the touch of Italian swords. The Italian flag, pride of Ausonia, is already fixed up on the Capitol.

Victory! Victory! Romans! Shortly you will see amidst you the hero of heroes; you are free, destiny is accomplished, Victor has shown you the path of glory!

Destiny is accomplished! Great, austere, splendid Rome, first glory of Italy, of the world, now redeemed thou art again the noble seat of Ausonia and of the king.

After a while, mounted on his impatient sorrel courser, fiercely neighing, proud on the saddle, quiet and happy Victor passes down the redeemed Roman streets amidst the plaudits, the cries, the hurrahs of an enthusiastic crowd, applauding, rejoicing;* and turning around his serene and assured eye predicts a future more beautiful and more proud. Arrived in the supreme hall, in the presence of all the great men of Italy, with rapid words and the hand upon the sword, "Gentlemen," he says, "the Italian star shines propitious! We are now in Rome, and here we will

---

* See chronicle about the entering of the king into Rome, on July, 1871.

remain !* Be this the supreme wish of my soul. This was the task which together with the frail crown I received at Novara from my loved father, king Charles Albert."

* * * * *

Is he dead ? Oh ! no ; Almighty God, thou wilt not take away from Italy such a glorious man ! · He is reposing in a placid and quiet sleep, and the body broken by cruel illness feels happy in this rest. No, he who in his heart nourished the holy fire of divinity cannot be mortal ! I see heaven send its prohibition to the work of death which is afraid in looking at this great monarch.

And yet the universal grief, the mourning which invades the soul, is already a tremendous proof of the unutterable deadly disaster. The people, dissolved in tears, already groan, and after the first a new afflicted crowd fills the road to the Quirinal, and arriving there find another lamenting crowd with bent eye and pain-stricken faces.

The ancestral walls of eternal Rome are covered with cloth ! Even the sky, always faithful to this race, to Italy and to his untamed people covers and veils. A large crowd of Seraphim, with golden hair, descend from high amidst us bringing to this great king the homage of the Eternal.

Alas ! the fatal tidings do not lie ! Victor, the father

---

* Historical words said at the opening of the first Parliament in Rome, on the 20th November, 1871.

of the country, the great Savoyard prince is dead ! Mourn Italy,—pour out freely thy sorrow.

Words cannot express such gigantic universal grief! and who dares to try to read the hidden will of God ?

In order to give him a greater reward he was pleased to take him away from this world, in the middle of the same Rome, which sealed his exploits, at the side of the weak old man adorned with the tiara, who once had blessed the flag and the arms of Italy, and in those same ancestral walls, the seat of glory, and the dream of all the ages.

O magnanimous example to all princes ! *Loyalty* had been his device ; *Love* the word which always was on his lips ! And how he loved his dear Italy ! What faith ! What pure and inviolate conscience ! What affection for his sons ! Humbert, thou well knowest it, thou who received the last royal farewell of thy parent ! Grief conquered thee, O king, and thou hadst cause for grief.

The words of this great one, when for the last time he turned his placid looks to the bystanders, all bent at his knees, and crying was, Italy ! Italy ! after which he rested silent for a while.

But when finally the minister of the Eternal came to him with the pledge of redemption and of pardon, certainly immersed in a supreme ecstacy, he asked mercy for all his actions. Mercy ? Proud were those actions, King Victor, and if it is true that Heaven is the reward given to the superhuman, thou rightly wilt sit at the side of God, and always looking down on us, on our actions, on

G

our longed-for destinies, wilt kindly watch us, O great father, founder of Italian greatness.

In every city of this happy land which thou hast made free from tyranny, may be raised a proud monument telling—Here is the great man who made us. Glory be to the worthy prince, to the first king of Italy !

And there amidst the old vaults of the Pantheon, where thou wilt find repose, many times I will come, father, to implore thee, and there from God, with fervid prayer, I will ask for Humbert's happiness, that he always may be as thou wast, great and loving, and for the sake of the angel that he leads at his side, for her that mother of Italy, already has gained the hearts of all her sons. I will always invoke his blessings, I will come with the living thought which boils in my youthful soul and quenches the fullness of my painful grief.

XVIII.

A SON.

TO MY FRIEND, C. A. MORPURGO.*

I.

WHEN they went to rent a room on the fifth flat, the porter, with a look full of contempt, understood all, and concluded—"Second rate people!" The youth with intelligent eyes was proud of his mourning on account of his new suit. His mother, already old at thirty years, hid under a thick black veil her large eyes red with tears, and when their goods, which were to be answerable for the rent, were brought in this poor lodging the porter became gloomy, and thought—"Quite second rate!" Nevertheless, as the rent was paid punctually, he corrected his words by—"Second rate but honest." And

---

* As a token of my continued friendship I dedicate to you this translation.

when he had noticed their manner of ringing the bell, for the sake of his dignity he never was in a hurry to open the door. The widow still had a lady-like appearance, and for her support gave lessons in singing. She always used to return home when her boy came back from school, and prepare his dinner. On Sunday they went together to the Luxembourg Gardens, threw some bread to the swans, and went home. It was one of those cases of respectable poverty in which if anybody tries to take an interest, he will receive a sweet smile, but no confidence. They pleased their neighbors, and the porter, bold at first, was by and by disarmed. Even he found some word of praise,—and when six years later one evening he became acquainted with the fact that the young man had gained all the prizes at the school, this father moved by such a zeal and courage thought, " Some day perhaps !......for our young miss !"......

Just the same day, when the young rhetorician, radiant with his own and also his mother's pride, showed to his mother for the twentieth time his prize, and embraced her vehemently, speaking to her on his knees, saying, "Mother how happy we are !" She suddenly taking his hands in hers, uttering from her heart all the hidden pains, confides all the bitterness of her life to her innocent, happy, and victorious boy.

She revealed to him how he had only his mother's name,—how in the eyes of the law she was not a widow. At the age of twenty she was earning her living by teaching singing. But why let a young girl go alone ? Old and worn-out story ! The singing mistress with the young gentleman. The criminal had died suddenly, without time for repairing his fault. She would have died at the same time, but she had a son. A son !

"Thou knowest the rest. This has been my deep sorrow for sixteen years. I am not in good health, my sight is going, thou hast no trade and we are in debt."

The boy had dreamed of glory,—of a sword,—of epaulettes,—a golden future,—and the greatest honour,—and now he would have to be satisfied with a thousand francs yearly. He began to comfort his mother, speaking to her as a man who is praying.

" Thou well knowest, we have a friend in the mairie;* he will give me employment; he is chief clerk. If only at twenty years I may draw a good number !† Why not? O yes, I am lucky in games, Mother be not sad. Beside, it is not for nothing that I am an artist. I can play the violin a little. One might make a profession of my drawing room accomplishment. I feel in my soul an indomitable courage,—you will see. Smile, then, mother, —smile. To begin with, *Madam*,‡ I will not be satisfied until you have smiled."

Poor, happy mother ! A tender smile for a moment lit up her sad face, and then, deeply moved, she drew to her breast her son and wept long, pressing him in her arms.

On the evening, the boy of seventeen years, left alone,

---

* The Government Buildings.

† In France, as well as in many other countries, the young have to draw a number, which will decide if they must go into active service.

‡ The boy showed his fictitious anger by calling his mother " Madam "

arranging with the others on the table his gilt edged
prizes said farewell to his former dreams,—and all the
rest went as he had foreseen. A very modest employment
occupied the day, and half of the evening was spent in
playing in a *café* concert, for he had truly said that any-
thing is useful to make a living. From the very day in
which he accepted the struggle he ceased to grow, and his
stature remained short as his ambition.

When the porter was aware of this resolution, offended
in his aristocratic feelings, he was not able to refrain from
criticism. "These second rate folks," he said, "have very
low instincts ; they might have risen—but had no per-
severence. Fancy my wife's having thought he might
do for our Emma; besides my daughter is destined for
the stage."

II.

And the good son learned the worry of office life,—the
long glance through the glass window at the free idler
who walks and smokes,—the loathing smell of the stove
to which surely a man gets used, but which still makes
one couch every morning,—the stupid joke at which one
must laugh,—the very common talk as to the feelings of
each toward the chief, and their hopes of an advance-
ment,—the monotonous and futile work,—and for the
only moment of breathing the fresh air whilst returning
to his lodgings with slow steps, enfeebled by hunger
which is badly satisfied by the unfailingly poor dinner.

Growing older, the mother had become soured,—truly

her misery and her long and painful virtue had been silent for a long time. The heart feels twice the pains it is obliged to keep secret. Besides she was ill ; finally her character seemed changed even to her dear son. By him the dinner time was abridged,—for himself as well as for her he suffered too much, seeing her begin some groundless complaint ; and always he left dinner as early as he could.

For the rest, at that hour duty called him to the suburb's little *café* concert, where every evening with his violin, behind the pianist leading the band without *batón*, and not far from a soldier puffing at the cornet, he listened distractedly, not amused at the painted singer with her bare shoulders,—the bearded baritone, embarassed in his white gloves,—and the *buffo* with his trembling and joined legs, with his high collar, making horrible grimaces, and narrating to the public his wedding day. At midnight only he got up and arrived at home ; sometimes he opened his books at his bed-side, but having no energy to read them, went to bed to spare the candle.

This life lasted five, ten, fifteen years. Alas ! fifteen times when the season of lilacs had returned he could see in the streets on Sunday evenings poor girls in fresh white dresses near the foot-path where indulgent parents sit, playing at shuttlecock with the young men. While always alone he kept away timidly,—he never passed near the pyramids of bowls filled with punch which adorn the counter of the *café*, where many times he had seen, as he passed, old bachelors, fond of unfeverish pleasures.

playing at dominoes with pipe in their mouth, calling each other "old chappie," and caressing their dogs.

He was envious of their lot, for this was his own, to earn his daily bread and his quarter's rent. In the first days when he was going to the orchestra a fair singer, half consumptive, cast on him a pitiful eye ; but he lowered his own every time she appeared on the stage. Later she passed on the other side of the Seine, and yet young died in the middle of *Quartier Breda*. Verily he had almost loved her, and kept the remembrance of the displeasure he felt, seeing her kiss and flirt with the actors ; and his profession became to him more painful than before.

III.

The health of his mother became worse. One night for her came death as sad as life had been ; and when they had carried her to the last resting place in deep mourning, and followed, as is the custom, by all his colleagues, happy at this holiday, he returned to his room—and alone began to think. He perceived himself without friends,—poor,—bachelor,—old before his time,—surprised at his grey hairs. He felt that his soul and his body for twenty years had taken the slow and growing habit of weariness, silence and solitude,—that he had pronounced only one word of love, "Mother !"—that he now had no hope to see a more tender chapter added to his very simple romance. Resigned but conquered, again he re-

turned by day to his office, in the evening to his desk—
and free he lived just as he used to live when a slave.
Even in the house where he lives nobody knows that he
exists; and at night, when he rings the bell, the old
porter, who now is seventy-two years old, and is losing
knowledge of things and of time, wakes up discontented
and murmurs in his lodge, " It is the boy of the fifth flat
who comes in !"

XIX.

THE TWIN SPIRITS.

TO MISS NORA HILLARY,

Teacher of Music.

I.

THE sun was near the end of its journey,—the air was filled with mystery,—the violets sent their odour to God,—the murmur of the stream was more lively,—all creation seemed to repeat the words òf love, and the heart was seized by a pious feeling which sweetly suggested prayer.

Prostrating myself before the rustic altar of the queen of heaven, a divine pity moved my soul, and I wept and prayed.

II.

Whilst to the throne of the Almighty, like a cloud of incense, joined to the sublime austere voice of the organ,

rose the prayer of the fervid worshippers so dear to him.
Suddenly I heard a sweet, strong, harmonious voice, which
troubled my heart and forced me to weep.

Raising my eyes appeared before me a young orator.
beautiful and divine in appearance, who struck my heart.

III.

For many and many days already the fair young man
had turned and returned around my house, looked at me
and smiled, and every day I saw his sweet image; blush-
ing, I too had answered the salute,—and each time he
came I lost my peace.

God grant that he may understand me as I understand
him ! And if he understand me and will give me his
heart I will adore him with an immense love.

IV.

He loves, yes, he loves me ! O celestial delight !—in
effable joy,—immense gladness ! No, this is not a dream
he has told me so, and his words are words of divine con-
sent. Yes, my beloved, I will love thee,—to thee I will
open all the most hidden recesses of my heart,—entirely
thine will be this my living soul. Sweetly, sweetly a
breath of love slightly touches my face. He has looked
at me......and has placed on my finger a ring,—a glittering circle of gold.

V.

See, see how the torches shine ! How beautiful is the altar festally adorned ! How many garlands ! How much incense, and how many lights ! O what a solemn function is this one ! How bright a day, and how the heaven's smile ! I will adorn my head with the nuptial crown. I will appear beautiful under my veil. Already the harmonious trumpet tune the joyful songs. O my faithful one ! dost thou not hear the people's outcries— " Hurrah ! for the bride !"

VI.

" Thou art married." So said the priest,—this old man thou knowest and who loves me so much ! Art thou then mine ? Wilt thou be always at my side ? Is then accomplished the hope of my heart ? But tell me, dear, why so sadly lookest thou at the ground and sighest ? What thought comes to abate the course of our joy ? Thinkest thou perhaps of thy mother, whom thou hast left alone ? We will go to her, but do not weep any more !

VII.

Three days are past, and yet he cannot come back ! Already three days,—three eternal days !—and I am dying ! My treasure has told me nothing. At dawn he kissed me, and quickly went away. Has he been to con-

sole his mother ?   But then he ought to return without
delay !   Pray, bright stars, bring him back to me.   Without my beloved I am failing, and I will preserve myself
alive for him, the only pride of my life, with whom I fell
in so great a love.

VIII.

Alas ! what are these melancholy voices,—this sad
sound of bells,—this grief which invades all the passers-
by ?   What wants this yet distant crowd ?   Somebody is
dead......and is accompanied to his home by weeping
faces !   Alas ! is it true—this my horrid vision ?   No,—
it cannot be true !   Eternal God, thou art not an unjust
punisher !   My mind is raving, and my thoughts are food
for my sorrows.

IX.

Yes, my love is dead !   The coloured cheeks have now
become pale, and the heart is silent.   The refulgent pupil
which before used to shine with divine ardour is now
closed.   God, why hast thou taken him, when scarcely
thou hadst granted me his sublime love ?   Like a little
flower which in the winter appears waving, and soon
after is leafless and dies, thou, my sweetheart, hast passed away.

X.

I am wretched, sad and alone, because they have taken
away my treasure, burying him under the green sod not

far from thy altar, Virgin Mary. They have laid on the coffin a few flowers,—singing pious songs. Prepare for me in the same place the nuptial bed. I come to thee my beloved, only comfort of my heart. United we will spread our wings to the celestial shore,—to the everlasting love.

At the last tolling of the sad bell well known to the village people, when the night has come, and the honest prayer of the peasant singing to the virgin ascends to the spheres,—when in the heaven rises the placid moon,—when the breezes become milder, and all around the universe is silent, adoring the Creator,—when on the branches the feathered birds tranquil hide their harmonious throats in their winged arms, and in the sky the most distant worlds reappear,—amidst the light vapours of the churchyard, a gentle flame towers alone and trembling for a while, finally rests and waits.

Not long after a sad and harmonious song is heard, and in the meanwhile one could see a like flame coming toward the first, and both, mingled in one embrace, sweetly disappear, like twins destined to the same fate, who felt immense joy in meeting each other.

The firm belief of the people is that the apparition is

the souls of the two unhappy ones who prematurely died in such great grief, and on account of this, the believer, pained for so great a misfortune, bows and weeping, says, *Ave Maria.**

---

* This Poem has been also translated into French, and has been admirably set to music by the *Maestro* GERVASIO, of Savona, conductor of the orchestra of the Theatre of Lyon.

HERE AND THERE THROUGH THE HISTORY OF ITALY.

A LECTURE

BY

A. A. NOBILE, B. A.,

Teacher of French and Italian.

FOLLOWED BY

MANZONI AND RATTAZZI,

AN ADDRESS BY THE SAME.

TORONTO:

J. S. WILLIAMS, PRINTER.

1884.

Baldwin, Right Rev. M. S., D.D., Bishop of Huron, (E.C.)
Ballentine, Mrs. C., Principal Somerville College, St. Clair
      Mich., U.S.
Beatty, W. H., M.P., Toronto.
Bendelari, Enrico, Esq., Vice-Consul of Italy, Toronto.
Berryman, Miss Cosie, Toronto.
Bethune, Rev. C. J. S.
Bethune, R. A., Esq., Toronto.
Biggar, C. R. W., Esq., Toronto.
Blake, Hon. E., Q.C., M.P., Toronto.
Blake, Hon. S. C., Q.C., Toronto.
Body, Rev. C. W. E., Provost Trinity College, Toronto.
Boddy, Ven. Samuel J., Arch Deacon, Toronto.
Bowes, Robert H., Esq., Toronto.
Boyd, Hon. J. A., Chancellor, Toronto.
Burke, Rev. J. W., Belleville.
Cameron, Mrs. Alexander, Toronto.
Cameron, John, Esq., Toronto.
Campbell, Hon. Sir A., Minister, Ottawa.
Carty, Miss Martha, Toronto.
Casey, Hon. G. W., M.P., Fingal.
Cassels, Hamilton. Esq., Toronto.
Cassels, Walter, Esq., Toronto.
Caven, Rev. W., Principal Knox College, Toronto,
Cayley, Rev. John D., Toronto.
Clark, Miss Elizabeth, Hamilton.
Clark, Rev. W., Prof. Trinity College, Toronto.
Clarke, Colonel E., Speaker Ontario Assembly, Toronto,
Cochran, Robert, Esq., Toronto.

Digby, James, M.D., Brantford.
Dixon, Rev. A., Guelph.
Dunfield, John, M.D., Petrolia.
Ellis, W. H., M.D., Prof. University.
Falconbridge, W. G., Esq.
Fava, Barone, Minister of Italy, Washington.
Fleming, Ch. E., Esq., Toronto.
Forster, Charles E., Esq., Washington.
Forster, W. A., Esq., Toronto.
Fulton, John, M.D., Prof. University.
Galt, Hon. T.
Geikie, W. B., M.D., Prof. University.
Giannelli, Cav. A. M., Consul-General of Italy, Montreal.
Gooderham, A., Esq., Toronto.
Gooderham, Henry, Esq., Toronto.
Gooderham, R. T. Esq., Toronto.
Graham, Moon, Esq., Postal Department, Ottawa.
Grant, George M., Very Rev., Kingston.
Gregg, Rev. W., Prof. Knox College, Toronto.
Grier, Miss Rose, Principal Bishop Strachan's School.
Gzowski, Colonel C. S., Toronto.
Hagarty, Hon. John H., Q C., Chief Justice, Toronto.
Hardagh, Hon. J. A., Judge, Barrie.
Haviland, Hon, T., Heath Governor, Prince Edward Island.
Hilliary, Miss Nora, Toronto.
Howland, Oliver A., Esq., Toronto.
Howland, W. H., Esq., Toronto.
Howland, Sir W. P., Toronto.
Hutton, Maurice, Prof. University, Toronto.
Johnson, Rev. H. B., D.D., Toronto.
Jones, Rev. W., Prof. Trinity College, Toronto.
Jones, Hon. T. J., Judge, Brantford.
Kerr, Rev. J., Durham.
Kirkland, Thomas, Prof., Toronto.
Kirkpatrick, Rev. J. W., Kingston,
Kirkpatrick, Hon. G. A., Speaker of the House, Ottawa.
Langton, Thomas, Esq., Toronto.
Langtry, Rev. John, Prof. University.

Lee, W. S., Esq., Toronto.
Lush, L. A., Q.C., Toronto.
Lyster, J., L.L.D., Kingston.
McLaren, Rev. W., Prof. Knox College, Toronto.
McMurrich, W. Barclay, Esq., Toronto.
Macdonald, Sir John A., Premier, Ottawa.
Macdonald, Grant, Esq., Toronto.
Macdonell, Rev. D. J., Toronto.
Maclennan, James, Q.C., Toronto.
Macnab, Rev. Alexander, Bowmanville.
Macoun, John, Prof., Ottawa.
Malloch, A. H., Esq., Toronto.
Meredith, Mrs. E. A., Toronto.
Moore, George J., Prof. Andower University, Mass., U.S.
Morden, A. L., Esq., Napanee.
Morris, Hon. Alex., M.P.P., Toronto.
Mowat Rev. J. B., Prof., Kingston.
Mowat, Hon. Oliver, Premier of Ontario.
Mulock, W., Esq., M.P., Toronto.
Nelles, Rev. S. S., President Victoria College, Cobourg.
Oldright, W., M.D., Toronto.
O'Mahoney, Right Rev. Timothy, D.D., Bishop, (R.C.)
Pardee, Hon. T. B., M.P., C.L.C., Toronto.
Patterson, Hon. Ch. S., Chief Justice.
Patterson, J. C., M.P., Ottawa.
Pinto, J., Esq., Chilian Legation, Washington.
Proudfoot, Hon. W., Toronto.
Richey, Hon. Matthew Henry, Governor of Nova Scotia.
Robinson, Hon. John B., Lieut. Governor of Ontario.
Robinson, Sir J. L., Toronto.
Rose, John E., Q.C., Toronto.
⁕ Rossi, Antonio, Toronto.
Scarth, Rev. A. C., Lennoxville.
Scarth, J L., Esq., Toronto.
Schneider, Rev. G. A. S., Prof Trinity College, Toronto.
Sheard, Charles, M.D., Prof. Trinity College, Toronto.
Smith, Goldwin, Prof. Toronto.
Spragge, Hon. J. Godfrey, Chief Justice, Toronto.

Stevenson, Rev. J. J., Montreal.
Sutherland, Rev. Alex., Toronto.
Sutherland, Rev. D. G., St. Thomas.
Sweetman, Rev. Arthur, D.D,, Bishop of Toronto, (E.C.)
Tane, Rev. Francis R., Bath.
Tilley, Hon. Sir Leonard, Minister, Ottawa.
Tindall, W., M.D., Washington.
Thomas, H. L., Esq., Translator Foreign Office, Washington
Tremayne, Rev. J., Mimico.
Tupper, Sir Charles, Minister, Ottawa.
Vandersmissen, W. A., Prof. University, Toronto.
Wild, Rev. Joseph, Toronto.
Williamson, Rev. James, Prof. Kingston.
Wilmot, Hon. Robert Duncan, Gov. New Brunswick.
Wilson, Daniel, L.L.D., Pres. University College, Toronto
Withrow, Rev. W. H., D.D., Toronto.
Workman, Joseph, M. D., Toronto.
Workman, J. C., Prof., Cobourg.
Wood, Hon. S. C., Toronto.
Wright, Robert R., M.A., Prof., Toronto.

In thanking you publicly for the patronage bestowed
on my MISCELLANEOUS POEMS, I hope you will kindly
patronize this my lecture and encourage my efforts.

I remain,

Yours obediently,

A. A. NOBILE.

HERE AND THERE THROUGH THE HISTORY OF ITALY.

Yet, Italy ! through every other land
   Thy wrongs should wring, and shall, from side to side ;
Mother of arts ! as once of arms ; thy hand
   Was then our guardian, and is still our guide,
Parent of our religion, whom the wide
Nations have knelt to for the keys of heaven !
   Europe, repentant of her parricide,
Shall yet redeem thee, and, all backward driven
   Roll the barbarian tide, and sue to be forgiven.
          Byron Child's Harold, Canto IV, Stanza 47.

WAS there ever a human being who, lifting up his eyes to the skies of Italy, could deny that there is the purest serene which God's smile has brightened ? These, ladies and gentlemen. are the words of one of our greatest contemporary writers, the late F. D. Guerrazzi, and for my part I do not believe they were presumptuous words. No, all those who have travelled through this country agree in saying that it is a paradise on earth. Lying between the blue waves of the Mediterranean and the Adriatic, backed by the sovereign Alps with their dark forests and ice-covered peaks, Italy is certainly majestic and great, but her predominant aspect is that of serene beauty. With a sky of the sweetest azure, with the mildest atmosphere, with a fertile soil, with a mantle of verdure, always fresh, covered with vineyards and olives, myrtles and aloes, all the Italian territory presents a rich and varied beauty. This scenery of Italy has been sung by the poets of every nation. Let me say in passing that I do not claim this sweet climate, and this blue heaven as an Italian virtue, but only as a gift given by the Almighty, for which we Italians ought to be grateful. It is this evening my intention and my duty to speak of something more worthy of our pride, I mean our history.

I will divide this my discourse into three parts. The first, beginning with the birth of Rome, will end with the establishment of Christianity, when Italy, under the name of Rome, was the world. The second, beginning at the fall of the Roman empire will end with the treaties of 1815. This is the epoch in which the Italian, like the *Israelitish people*, were the slaves of domestic or foreign tyrants. The third part will describe the struggle of Italy to obtain her independence. Allow me your kind attention, and excuse my bad pronunciation.

Very little I will tell you about the first epoch, with which you are all familiar. Every educated man could not have done less than read and study the history of the Roman republic and empire. The culture of Egypt and Greece was inherited by Rome. The Roman eagles conquered the world, and everywhere brought civilization. Travel if you like over all the old world, from the high mountains of Scotland to the burning sands of Africa, from Spain to the Euphrates, you will see the remains of the Roman power. Thinking of, or going to Rome, the mind of every civilized man cannot but think of the famous names of Cammillus and Cincinnatus, of the Scipios and Caesars. Yes, ladies and gentlemen, when Britain, Gaul, Germany, and Spain were yet sleeping in darkness and ignorance, the Roman Capitol resounded with the shouts of the triumphant legions, the forum resounded with the noble words of the tribunes and the Gracchi, and the senate, silent and attentive, listened to the orations of Cicero and Cato. The same Rome that had destroyed her rival Carthage, that had outlived the conquests of the great Alexander, that in culture and learning had surpassed ancient Egypt, arrived at the acme of her greatness, swaying her sceptre over a population of 120,000,000, by degrees lost her strength. Her conquered provinces not only rebelled themselves, but in their turn became conquerors, and with the dissappearance of the Roman empire begins the second period.

Christianity first found an asylum in Rome. There in the first days of the church thousands of persons, converted from heathenism to the religion of the cross, gave their lives in its defence. There took place a terrible struggle between heathenism and Christianity, when at last the latter seated herself on the throne of the Caesars, acquiring a dominion larger than theirs. But if the establishment of Christianity in Rome gave her an unlimited moral power over the world, it destroyed also the remains of the Roman empire. The north came into the possession of thousands of barbarians, called Goths,

Visigoths, Longobards, Gauls; while the south was more especially the prey of Moors and Spaniards. In the middle of Italy sprang up thousands of little duchies and republics.

It is not my intention to relate to you to-night the deeds of this epoch; it is a very sad history. I will only say that in the midst of her intestine discords, in her feebleness and decay, lying under the iron hoof of France, Germany, or Spain, Italy remained always the seat of beauty, the land of poetry and song, the cradle of every beautiful form and divine melody.

If the sons of the Romans bathed themselves in their brethren's blood, if they were ruled by ecclesiastical or civil tyrants, no one could take from her hands the sceptre of genius. In this beautiful peninsula the juris-consult expounded those principles which form the basis of the jurisprudence of all European nations. Navigators like Columbus and Amerigus added a new world to the boundaries of the old one, and the learned discovered the treasures of antiquity. There sang Dante, Tasso, Ariosto and Petrarch, there Raphael, Michael Angelo, Ciotto, Leonardo, da Vinci painted with celestial colors, there Macchiavelli and Vico speculated, and there Galileo studied beneath the open sky.

To speak to you to-night of the phalanx of Italian celebrities of this second epoch would require volumes, and besides it would be impossible. From these I have selected three, of whom I shall speak a few words. I mean Dante, the father of Italian poetry, Macchiavelli, the prince of politicians, and the great Galileo.

DANTE was born at Florence in the year 1265, sixty-three years before the birth of Chaucer, the morning star of English poetry. Boccaccio has left us his portraiture. " He was," said he, " of middle height, with oblong face, aquiline nose, large eyes, dark complexion, hair and beard dark and bushy, his demeanor was thoughtful and sad, his bearing grave, and his manners cultivated."

At the age of eighteen years he had already shown such a genius for poetry as to have gained the friendship of the most illustrious men. Though young, he was honored with one of the highest offices of the city, called *priore*. He was chosen to serve on no less than fourteen embassies, and sent to different places, and it is said that nothing of importance was done in Florence without consulting him.

Having exiled from Florence the Guelphs, or partisans of the Pope, when Charles of Valois made himself master of the said city, in his turn he was banished with the other Ghibelins. Exile was not his only punishment, but he was fined 8,000 lire, and in case this sum should not be paid in a fixed time, his property was to be confiscated, and his house burned. The 10th of May, of the same year, this sentence was confirmed, with the addition that if he himself had the misfortune to fall into the hands of the government, he should perish at the stake. For nineteen long years Dante longed for his beloved Florence without daring to approach its gates. Oh ! how hard and painful this privation seemed to the poor exile ! How much he suffered ! How often he was tortured by hunger, and tasted.—

Come sa di sale
Lo pane altrui, e quant' è dura cosa
Lo scendere e 'l salir per l' altrui scale. *

Dante wrote much, but nothing surpassed his poem, " The Divine Comedy; or, the Vision of Hell, Purgatory and Paradise." Certainly among the great beauties with which this fiction is filled, in our days we are sometimes shocked at some strange sentiments, at some superstitious ideas, at some atrocious bigotry, which we find in it. This is not the fault of the poet, but of the century in which he wrote. Without fear of being contradicted, I will add something more,—that for his epoch Dante was an advanced liberal. In this civilized century we should think it ridiculous to see innocent children regarded as infidels, and condemned to hell, only because they have not received the rite of baptism, while the perse-cutors of progress—as cruel or more cruel than Nero —were in celestial glory. Notwithstanding, his poem is sublime ; and all that he describes, horrible or ludicrous, beautiful or ugly, all seems real and true, so well does he present it to us. Dante was not only the creator of his allegory, but he created also the Italian language, which, at his epoch, existed only in a state of rudeness and im-perfection. He was the first to give it strength and beauty.

---

* Thou wilt prove how bitter is the bread of charity, and how weary it is to wait in the ante-chambers of the great.

Dante loved, with a pure love, Beatrice Portanare, a woman already married, and who died very young. Dante could never take her from his heart, and her image, her memory, gave him new life. He chose her as the polar star of his destiny. With her he ascended to Paradise.

I will not speak of his book " The Monarchy," a work considered by somebody as a complete Utopia, and in which he tries to prove that, according to God's will, a universal monarchy was necessary to universal peace,— and that this monarchy, by justice and divine will, was the Roman one ; declaring Rome to be the city destined by God to be the universal apostolic throne.

In his exile Dante repaired to Verone, where he worked at his Poem, and where he was not happy. Petrarch narrates how he had a dislike to one of the courtiers who, on account of his wit and buffooneries, was the favorite. The prince Can della Scala one day asked Dante how it happened that such a fool could make himself welcome, while he, so learned and wise, could not succeed. He quickly answered, " Your highness would not be so much astonished if you would consider that friendship is produced by similarity of ideas and feelings."

From Verona, Dante went to Ravenna. In the year 1320 he was sent as ambassador to Venice, but he failed in obtaining even an audience, which worried him very much. A few days after his return from this embassy, he died in his fifty-sixth year, and in the nineteenth year of exile.

Three years before his death he could have returned to Florence, but he rightly scorned every offer of pardon which would offend his pride and dignity. I will quote a passage from one of his letters. "I hear," he writes, "from your letters and those of my nephews and other friends that I could take advantage of the decree proclaimed in favor of the return of the exiles, that is, that paying a certain sum and submitting myself to the ceremony of being presented, I would also be absolved and return. This proposition implies two things that seem ridiculous and ill advised to those who have spoken to me of it, in regard to which you, more wise and discreet, have said nothing. Would this then be the glorious return of Dante Alighieri after very nearly fifteen years of sufferings and of exile? My innocence known to everybody deserves it? For this I shall have studied and sweated, etc."

As generally happens, Florence having heard of the death of Dante repented of her cruelty, and sent to Ravenna embassy upon embassy to claim his remains. Forty years afterwards Florence returned to the family the confiscated properties, and two centuries later the greatest fame and honors were granted to him who had lived with suffering and died in exile.

To-day in that Italy forming one kingdom from Alps to Sicily, the memory of the Ghibelin poet is venerated more than ever, and I shall never forget the feast on occasion of the centenary of his birth. All the Italian cities had sent a deputation to Florence which was filled with joy and fraternal gaiety.

Macchiavelli was a great politician and a profound thinker. The history of Florence written by him is one of his best books. Although dedicated to a pope, he did not hide or spare the papal folly and usurpations. He shows how Theodosius, King of the Goths, by shifting his court to Ravenna, gave to the bishop of Rome the occasion to strengthen his temporal power by means of alliances with the foreigners, generating jealousies and animosity between the popes and the emperors, and originating all those wars and dissensions which agitated Italy for centuries,—" So that all the wars," he says, " that hereafter the foreigners had with Italy were specially caused by the popes," and many of the barbarian hordes which poured into Italy were in great part due to the intrigues and excitement of the popes, and this course of action then taken, and since pursued, has' kept and still keeps Italy feeble and divided. The book " The Prince " has procured for Macchiavelli the reputation of a great intriguer. For my part I agree completely with Lord Bacon, when he says that we owe a great deal of gratitude to Macchiavelli for having exposed what men do, instead of telling us what they ought to do.

Macchiavelli praises the scheme of the Borgia to destroy and master the counts and princes, who were leagued with him, and with whom just then he had signed a treaty of friendship and peace, adopting the jesuitical maxim that " the end justifies the means." " Generally," he says, " virtue ought to be preferred to vice, but in special cases vice itself might become a virtue when asserted in a good cause."

In the year 1852, when Napoleon III betrayed the republic, then we heard the same mode of argument employed by his defenders. "Yes," they say, "it would have been right and honest if he had not committed this infamy; but for his own sake and for sake of the country intrusted to him, he acted well in becoming a criminal and a perjurer.

Macchiavelli could not avoid persecutions, and being suspected of having taken a part in a conspiracy, he was tortured; but while his body was suffering—not a moan, not a single word escaped his lips. He ended his days poor and neglected.

GALILEO was born at Pisa on the 15th of February, 1564. He was not a poet nor a statesman, but a thinker and a learned man. He began his career at Padua, where, if he did not invent, he perfected the compass, the telescope, and the microscope. He discovered the satellites of Jupiter, and gave them the name of "Medicean stars." Ferdinand, Grand Duke of Tuscany, offered him a chair in the University of Pisa, with leave to sojourn in Florence, and with no obligation of lecturing. In his first visit to Rome he made a new discovery, which appeared very extraordinary,—namely, the dark spots of the sun. In the year 1620 Galileo finished his great work, "Dialogues on the Ptolomaic and Copernican System." In the year 1624 Galileo returned to Rome to compliment the new Pope, Urban VIII, on the occasion of his elevation to the Papal Throne. His sojourn in the above mentioned city was not prolonged beyond two months, and in this lapse of time he had six long and satisfactory

audiences with the Pope, receiving, at his departure, many
presents and the promise of a pension for his son.

In 1632 the aforesaid book was published, accompanied
by a dedication to Ferdinand Medici. In this work he
explains and proves, with the clearest demonstrations, the
movement of the earth. The clergy and Pope Urban VIII
who had already adopted the system of Ptolomy, and who
fancied they ought to stand or fall with it, could not bear
the independent mind of Galileo ; and after much hesita-
tion not to offend the Grand Duke, Galileo's protector,
the book was finally condemned, and the writer summon-
ed to the Roman court. He arrived in Rome on the six-
teenth February, 1633, and Cardinal Barberini, one of his
friends and admirers, advised him to remain continually
in the house of Niccolini, Tuscany's ambassador, refusing
all visits, even those of his dearest friends. When the
time came to be examined, he was lodged in the apart-
ment of the treasury of the Inquisition, and if for a while
we ponder on the habits of this infamous tribunal, we
must confess that he was treated with unusual leniency.
His proud spirit, nevertheless, was bent by the threats of
dreadful anathemas. On the 20th June, four months
after his arrival in Rome, he was again brought to the
holy office, and the following day, dressed as a penitent,
with only his shirt on, he was accompanied to the convent
of Minerva, where the prelates and cardinals were assembled to pronounce his sentence ; and after having
kneeled, he recanted the principles he had taught, saying in a subdued voice, " *and yet it moves.*" Four days
after this recantation he was released from prison and

returned to his villa in Arcetri. Taken ill, he asked permission to go to Florence to consult some renowned doctors, but his petition was refused. A few years after the inquisitor Fariano wrote to him that the Pope would allow him to go to Florence, provided he would never go in the streets, nor receive his friends, and this order was carried out so severely that even in Passion Week he had to ask for a special permission to go to Mass. A few years afterwards he became blind, and in the year 1642, he died at the age of 78 years, in the arms of Viviani his loved pupil.

Galileo was broad shouldered, well proportioned, and of little more than the ordinary height; his complexion was beautiful and ruddy, his eyes lively, and his hair reddish. He was very fond of society, and his gentle and kind manners had made him welcome amongst all those who were acquainted with him. Having died a prisoner of the Inquisition, the Pope contested his right to make a will, and for this same reason he was buried in a dark corner of Santa Croce, although a large amount of money had been collected to raise him a monument.

Here, ladies and gentlemen, before entering into the third part of my lecture, I shall make only two short observations.

The first is that, from what I have already said, you will have observed that these three geniuses of Italy had to suffer from the real enemies of all progress. Unhappily they were not alone, but they had a thousand companions, martyrs to science and progressive ideas.

The second observation is that, although they died

poor, to-day in the Church of Santa Croce, in Florence, anyone can see the splendid monuments erected to their memories. Late justice, you will say; yes, late, but better late than never, and then this observation ought to encourage us to do all we can for the moral and social progress of humanity.

I have now arrived at my third period. The three kingdoms of England, Ireland and Scotland had formed only one government. The iron hand of Richelieu had joined into one France the different kingdoms of Brittany, Picardy, Provence, etc. The French conqueror emulous of Alexander and Cæsar, after having sacrificed thousands of victims, after having disturbed the peace of all the powers for the second time was defeated at Waterloo. The nations which had formed the Holy Alliance had in conference signed the treaty of 1815. Those diplomatists, those gentlemen, without consulting the will of the people had inter-changed millions of subjects. Austria had taken two of the richest Italian Provinces, Lombardy and Venice. The wife of the fallen Cæsar was destined to rule the little duchy of Parma. In this way Italy was divided into nine different principalities. Besides the insignificant but happy republic of *San Marino* there were in Italy eight petty tyrants joined together to oppose the people and to take away from them what they could. A great desire to see their country free, united and powerful began to work amongst the Italians. All the well educated and clever men were of this opinion, but the means of arriving at this union and independence were completely different. The greatest part expected everything from their own governments. The Italian poets kept on exciting the people to hatred of the foreigners, and to unite their force against their oppressors.

Niccolini, Pellico, Berchet, Giusti, Gioberti and Cavour, Mazzini and Garibaldi, although of different opinions, had dedicated their lives to the deliverence of their country. This is the epoch over which I like to linger, because it reminds me of the accomplishment of our hopes. The eight little despots were entirely masters of the situation, when a man with the watchword "God and the people," put himself at the head of a persistent movement. Let the political or religious adversaries of Mazzini say what they like, it is my firm opinion that if we have now a United Italy, the greatest honour is due to Joseph Mazzini. This man at the age of two-and-twenty years was arrested under suspicion of being one of the *Carbonari*, by order of Charles Albert, who himself had been a chief of this society, and after having remained for six months in the fortress of Savona, without trial, was condemned to perpetual exile, being granted as a special grace, the favour of a three hours' interview with his mother before leaving the country. He went to Marseilles, where, perceiving the defects of *Carbonarismo*, namely, that it was not fit to educate and organize for the very simple reason that it had neither unity, nor principles, nor creed, nor faith, nor watchword, he found a new patriotic secret society, called "Young Italy," and in order to propagate and strengthen it, he began the publication of a new weekly paper, the organ of his party, and

bearing the same name. In the columns of this news-
paper he showed so great talents and such profound
knowledge of the necessities of his country, that irre-
sistibly he attracted to his ideas the best of the youth,
who recognized soon in him their chief.

Several revolutionary movements, attempted by the
followers of Mazzini, took place, but being unassisted, of
course they were always repulsed. Everywhere the
leaders were sentenced to death, and imprisonment in
fortresses. Those who were put to death ascended the
scaffold courageously, and died with the words of "Italia
Una" on their lips.

The cause of Italian independence, like the cause of the
first Christians, acquired strength. For every new martyr,
a hundred courageous proselytes presented themselves.
In the year 1848 a great movement took place all over
Europe. People asked for reforms. The French throne
fell, and instead of it the Republic was proclaimed. Who
fought the famous "five days" of the Milanese revolution? Did not the men belonging to the society of Young
Italy? Without arms they exposed their lives, they
fought, and they expelled from the walls of the city a
powerful army. From north to south Italians asked for
reforms. The king of Piedmont gave a constitution, and
was imitated by the Grand Duke of Tuscany and the
king of the Two Sicilies. All joined with the Pope in
declaring war against Austria, the common foe. The en-
thusiasm was general. I was then at college in Pisa, and
I cannot forget the joy with which a companion of mine,

B

who was departing with the battalion of the students, came to bid me good-bye. "Adieu," he said, "if I die, I will meet thee in heaven." Poor Charles ! * Thy foreboding has been fulfilled ; thou wast killed by the oppressor's bullet. What is to be hoped for from leaders who do not truly wish for the good of the country ? The Pope, the Grand Duke of Tuscany, and the king of the Two Sicilies were not sincere. What became of their armies ? The Romans, although blessed by the infallible, were obliged to capitulate at Vicenza ; the Neapolitans were called back by the king to be employed in murdering and massacreing their own brethren, and the Tuscans, Lombards and Piedmontese were defeated at Curtatone and Novara. The king Charles Albert and his two sons fought bravely.

The battle ended, the king asked if he could have ten thousand fresh troops to open a passage and retire to Alexandria. Having received a negative answer, he assembled the different generals and spoke thus, "For eighteen years I tried to procure the happiness of my people. I am pained to see all my hopes deluded. To-day it was impossible for me to die on the battle-field as was my ardent wish. Perhaps my presence would be an obstacle in obtaining from the enemy honorable conditions, and moreover I cannot continue the war. I abdicate then my crown in favour of my son Victor Emmanuel." The new king met with Marechal Radetski, who,

---

* Charles Vincenti, a Corsican, my companion in college at Lucca, was killed at the battle of Curtatone.

amongst other conditions, asked for the abolition of the constitution and the alliance with Austria.

To these proposals Victor Emmanuel, filled with wrath, answered, "Marechal, before I sign these conditions I would lose not one but a hundred crowns. Is then your wish for a deadly struggle ? Let it be, you shall see of what revolution the little Piedmont will be capable. My family knows very well the road to exile, but not the road of dishonour."

Here to exonerate Charles Albert from the name of traitor, given him by a few, I will cite his last words, spoken to General Santa-Rosa at the moment the ex-king was leaving for Portugal where he intended to sojourn, and where he afterwards died. "I go," he said, "but at the first war that Austria will have she will be sure to find me in the first files of its enemies." How could a traitor pronounce such generous words ?

The Italian nation tried to act by herself. The flag of hope, the flag of Dio e Popolo, floated over the bulwarks of brave Venice during the hardship of the few months of her siege. But where the Italians showed of what they were capable of when treated like free men was at Rome, where under the orders of Rosselli, Avezzana and Garibaldi, an army of 14,000 men, spread over a district to defend which would have needed a force of at least 50,000, with ruined fortresses, kept at bay an army of 30,000 French troops. Nevertheless, both Rome and Venice were forced to surrender.

Let the enemies or detractors of Italy narrate what they please, they cannot change these facts, that the

Roman republic was proclaimed on the 9th day of February, 1849, some weeks before Mazzini entered Rome, that it was proclaimed by an assembly of 144 members, all of whom, except one, were Romans, that the total number of the troops under Generals Avezzana, Rosselli and Garibaldi was 14,000 men, all of whom, except 1,4000, were subjects of the Pope. This is the pure truth, and ought to be enough to answer the slanders and calumnies of the Ultramontanists and clericals who are writing and saying that foreign vagabonds, guided by Mazzini and Garibaldi founded the Roman republic.* No, ladies and gentlemen, every attempt made by those Ultramontanists to insult with falsehood and lies the Roman republic, which lasted only a few months, must fall before the strong logic of facts.

The hour of Italian independence had not yet arrived. The French republic from which Rome expected so much was the murderer of the Italian republics, and all the efforts made by the last two ended by a return to the *statu quo*.

Piedmont was the only state which kept its constitution. The new king by opening his kingdom to every proscribed person, and by helping them, acquired their sympathy, and the right of their confidence and gratitude. The constitution was found useful, the people and the king became used to this form of government. The Piedmontese parliament, with Cavour, Siccardi, Rattazzi,

---

* With more reason we could say that of the fanatics every nation formed the foreign mercenaries who were the defenders of the Pope-king.

Brofferio, and so many others, made useful laws, and the new liberals, having faith in Victor Emmanuel, worked with their absent brethren, the followers of Mazzini, for the same end, but by different means.

A formidable power threatened the peace of Europe. France, England and Turkey allied themselves against this colossus. Not from necessity, but only as a political demonstration, these powers asked the co-operation of Piedmont and the kingdom of the Two Sicilies. While Cavour, the minister of the first of these two states, willingly sent 25,000 men, under the orders of General Lamarmora, the king Bomba, the murderer of so many innocents, refused his help under the plea of great affection for his subjects. Oh! ladies and gentlemen, certainly God moved with pity at the Italian sufferings, permitted the refusal of the Neapolitan minister. After the fall of Sebastopol, Piedmont was called to send a plenipotentiary to the congress which was to be convened, for discussing the conditions of the peace. On this mission was sent Cavour, who so well represented the wishes of the Italians, and who so well conciliated the sympathies of the western powers, telling them of the tyranny of Austria and the Two Sicilies, both neutral in the last war.

What would have happened if the king of Naples had sent his troops to the Crimea? Probably he would have had his own ambassador, and then—God knows. The past is past and we have to be grateful to God who granted us a king like Victor Emmanuel, a stateman like Cavour, and generals like La Marmora and Garibaldi.

Little Piedmont, under the ministry of Cavour, gained

the sympathy of the other nations by a government truly constitutional and liberal. Austria, seeing that he marched with progressive ideas, proudly ordered him to disband the volunteers. Cavour was no longer isolated. At Plombières he had made an ally. Austria declared war, but behind little Piedmont she found all the Italian patriots and France, who by land and sea sent a hundred thousand soldiers.

At the news of the declaration of war the Grand Duke of Tuscany was obliged to leave his state. Without any bloodshed a provisional government was constituted, and it was ordered that the troops should march with the French and Piedmontese, forming the 5th army corps, under the orders of Prince Jèrome Napoleon. Piedmont opened an enlistment of volunteers, and they came in such numbers that the formation of another independent corps was deemed necessary, and General Garibaldi was destined to command it. The choice could not have been more fortunate ; all the youth went to join him. He was ably seconded by the Colonels Cosenz, Medici and Bixio. The Emperor Napoleon in his proclamation to the French nation had promised to make Italy free from the Alps to the Adriatic.

Austria was vanquished at Solferino, the road to Venice was free, and when all were hoping to see the programme maintained, when already every heart longed for the pleasure of extending freedom to their brethren of Venice, who had fought so well in 1849,—like a thunderclap came the news that the two emperors Francis Joseph and Napoleon III, without consulting Victor Emmanuel, had signed a truce. This news excited the anger of the Italians, anger which became rage when they were informed tnat Piedmont had acquired Lombardy, but would have to give up Nice, the birth-place of Garibaldi, and Savoy, the cradle of the royal family.

It is true that there was a clause—that the will of the people should be consulted, but alas! the vote was affirmative, and Nice and Savoy were lost for Italy. Mazzini protested, but on this, as well as other occasions, he stood alone; and we will here notice with admiration the practical sense of the Italians who, for the public good, were ready to renounce party spirit. In this same year, 1859, with the Lombardy were also annexed the Granduchy of Tuscany, the Duchies of Parma and Modena, with some papal provinces.

Garibaldi could not remain inactive, and, aided by Cavour, he went to the succour of the Sicilian patriots who had rebelled in the mountains. The Neapolitan army was 200,000 strong, under the protection of the Immaculate Conception, and yet Garibaldi landed with a thousand ex-communicated men. After two battles he entered Palermo, where soldiers came not only from Italy but from every part of the world. The Generals Cosenz, Medici and Bixio were again with him. Having crossed Calabria, Garibaldi, on the 8th of September, entered Naples alone, and was received with joy, while the king retired to Capua. After two months of siege, Capua yielded. The Italian government sent to Naples a governor, the people were consulted, and they voted annexation to the Italian kingdom.

Certainly Italy had made great progress towards her unity, but the possession of Rome, the natural capital, was earnestly desired by Garibaldi, who tried to organize a new expedition. The Italian troops, forced by an order from France accompanied by threats of war in case of disobedience, went against the general. Notwithstanding the desire of Garibaldi not to shed the blood of brethren the troops fired and he himself was wounded. The grief was universal in Italy, but what could the new-born nation do ? Avenge him and destroy all that had been done ? No, certainly, they had to suffer and be patient.

In the year 1866 the obstinate patriot again endeavoured to go to Rome, put this time instead of the Italian troops he found the Don Quixote of the Pope, the brave general de Failly. who afterwards, in 1870, had not the courage to fight with the Prussians, but who on this occasion tried his *merveilleux chassepots* upon a few badly organized but courageous patriots.

Again Europe was attracted by the sound of the war-like clarions. Two powers, which like vultures, had fallen on little Denmark were to come in conflict. Always watchful for every occasion favourable to her unity, Italy allied with Prussia against her common foe—Austria. Either through ignorance or by the mistake of our chiefs, although the army fought bravely, we lost the battle of

---

* Les chassepots firent merveilles -'The chassepots have done wonders— *Words of General De Failly's Report.*

In the French language, as well as any other language, the deadly weapons never *do wonders,* inasmuch as death is always a misfortune, and speaks of sadness and not of wonder. General de Failly undertook to be witty, otherwise he would have chosen other word.

Custoza and Lissa. At the end of the war, after the defeat at Sadowa, Italy obtained Venice and the Quadrilatero.

We have seen that the possession of Rome was the aim of the Italians, and how France would not allow Italy to occupy that city, and how Italy, either from fear of war or through gratitude, was obedient to the former. But it was written in the eternal pages of destiny that France indirectly should surrender Rome, in spite of the famous *jamais* (never) of Rouher.

When least expected, discord, for a very trifle, kindled a flame between Prussia and France. By both of these governments Italy was urged to form an alliance, but she preferred to be neutral and to mind her own affairs. The French troops destined for the Pope's protection were recalled from Rome. Alas! what will be the fate of the Infallable left alone in the midst of a wicked excommunicated nation? Ladies and gentlemen, the glorious defenders, the papal *zouaves*, together with the affection and love of his subjects, will be enough to defend him. Yes, if this love and this affection had truly existed, Rome perhaps might have been defended; unhappily for him, and happily for us, this great love for the murderer of Monti and Tognetti existed only in the brain of a few of his flatterers and supporters. The Italian army took possession of the holy city with very little bloodshed, and since this epoch the Pope is a *poor prisoner on straw* in his beautiful Vatican, in the hand of the sacrilegious Italian, as safe and well as he was before. Here, ladies and gentlemen, ends the struggle between independence

and slavery, and finally Italy has proclaimed her right-
to sit at the councils of the nations. To-day she has civil
and religious freedom, and is no more as Dante said,—

" *Non donna di provincie, ma bordello.*"

To-day, Italy is a land of life and energy, and knows
well how to progress. I am happy to speak before a
people who have usually shown great sympathy for our
country. What will be the destiny of this nation ? It is
in the hands of God; and none can tear off the veil
which hides it. We have reason to believe it will be
great. The king, Victor Emmanuel, is beloved ;* and a
liberal constitution gives the means of diminishing the
very large public debt and of improving the education of
the people. With economy, Italy will succeed in abolish-
ing many rather heavy taxes. Being peninsular, for her
defence she only needs a strong fleet and naval fortresses.
An army of 200,000 in the north will be enough to defend
her in case of war.

It is not without reason that at the beginning of my
lecture I quoted a stanza of the immortal Byron. Certainly when he wrote—

> Europe repentant of her parricide,
> Shall yet redeem thee.

He only intended to express a wish ; this wish at the
same time has proved a prophecy. England, France,

---

* Since the time of my lecture the faithful king, Victor Emmanuel, has
gone to receive the recompense due to his virtues. His son Humbert the
First is also loved, and successor to the throne, is also the successor of his
father's love for Italy.

Prussia have all given their moral or material support to Italian independence. Yes, Italy now is redeemed, the noble wish of Byron has been satisfied. Let me also to-night express from the depth of my heart a wish which I hope will be shared by all present.

May Italy, so long the seat of religious persecutions, which once desolated the earth, under a free government create a new people whose glory shall be the gospel stripped of all superstitions, a people whose liberty shall give birth to equality and tolerance of every form of worship. Let us wish that my countrymen will try especially to educate themselves, so that everyone may vote* and know how to vote. Then the sons of Italy again raising their heads, and with the tri-color floating over them, march proudly onward in the consciousness of their own and their ancestor's glory, shouting aloud like them

CIVIS ITALICUS SUM.

---

* This wish has also been in part fulfilled. Although not as extensive as I would have it, a new electoral law has given a vote to many more thousand persons. This law I hope will be extended as soon as the people will have improved in education and learning.

MANZONI AND RATTAZZI.

AN ADDRESS DELIVERED BY SIGNOR A. A. NOBILE, ON THE 18TH OF JULY, 1873.

LADIES AND GENTLEMEN,

  The inexorable scythe of time, at little distance from one another, has cut down two illustrious lives. Two men whose renown will last as long as the world, left the earth and took their flight toward the sublime regions, appointed for those who have made themselves useful to their fatherland.

  ALEXANDER MANZONI and URBANO RATTAZZI are no more. The cultivated, learned and great poet, with the lawyer and eloquent orator, have departed, leaving every true Italian sad and doleful for their loss. Having the honour to present myself to you, it has been suggested to me to say a few words about those men of genius,—both dear to our Italy, but in a different way. I accepted the charge, but how do I feel now the burden of this under-taking. Where shall I find in my meagre knowledge language sufficient to set forth the virtues and merits of our contemporaries ? With what courage shall I, new to the platform of the lecturer, dare to narrate to you their actions ? I tremble at this responsibility, especially on account of the shortness of the time assigned to me ; but it is a sweet comfort to know that you all, ladies and gentlemen, assembled here, will show yourselves indulgent ; and giving me credit for my good intentions, will hear what I have to say with that gentleness and kindness which always formed and now forms a part of your character.

ALEXANDER MANZONI was born in Milano. His life offers to the biographer very few romantic incidents. While young he was attracted toward the ideas of Voltaire, but his sympathy for them did not last long, and soon he became an ardent and sincere follower of the Catholic faith. It is the opinion of many that to be liberal entails the consequence of being an anti-catholic—ALEXANDER MANZONI was a proof to the contrary. Who would deny to the illustrious writer the qualification of an Italian liberal citizen ? In reading his works, in going over his pages do we not find everywhere clear and manifest hatred of foreign invasion, pain at the chains with which Italy was fettered, and hope to see his country one, great and religious ? If religion inspired Manzoni with the hymns of the Passion, Pentecost and Christmas, his lively love of the fatherland inspired him also with the ode to Theodore Koerner and with the chorus of Carmagnola ! Who amongst us has not read at some time the Betrothed? How do we not tremble with rage in considering the arrogance of Rodrigus and the *Innominato*, backed by the *bravi*, in that unhappy epoch of civil dissensions ? Who of you does not feel sad and moved at the misfortunes suffered by the two lovers *Lucia* and *Renzo* ? Are not the two characters of Father Christopher and Cardinal Borromeo a beautiful lesson and a silent reproach to the Italian clergy ? What sensible man would dare to speak evil, or to curse a religion whose ministers were like the above-named, full of zeal, charity, love towards their neighbors, and self-denial ? Yes, ladies and gentlemen, it was Manzoni's belief, and it is also mine, that one can be a good citizen, remaining at the same time a good catholic. Manzoni knew how to be one, and when he saw that the Italian priest, forgetting his fatherland, made himself an obstinate supporter of slavery and ridiculous dogmas so far from the true ideal of Catholicism, he forsook the church, and scorning the excommunications of the Vatican, followed his king to Rome. He remained a good catholic at heart and in his actions, but left the iniquitous and false who, with their deeds, made hateful to the people a religion founded on charity, love and forgiveness.

Some will be astonished that Ma zoni, even after the famous five days of Milano, could remain in that city without being molested by the tyranny of the victorious oppressors. Gentlemen, Manzoni who by his writings has contributed t the freedom of Italy, was never a conspirator, and kept himself aloof from the militant politic, and neither Giulay nor Radetsky could have dared to molest a man eminently honest and patriotic. Virtue is respected even by its enemies. What can I say of the works of this great writer ? Besides those already mentioned I will cite the Adelchi, the Carmagnola of which, by-and-by, I shall recite the chorus. Nor shall I forget the ode of the 5th of May, in praise of him who had reached, if not surpassed, the renown of Cæsar and Alexander, I mean the great Napoleon—dead at St. Helena. Was it true glory ? Sublime question, which the future will answer, when, as Berchet said,

> Sopra il lutto espiato dai lutti,
> Il perdono e l' obblio correrà.*

When the progress shall have abolished war, scourge of the world, ruin of the nations, and shall have joined the people in one tie of brotherly friendship. Utopia, somebody will answer, Utopia, let it be, but a sweet and consoling Utopia. In his last words Manzoni summed up the motive of all his life. " Pray," he said, " for the king and his family, so good to us." Manzoni, at the age of eighty years, thou didst die,—it was necessary to pay thy tributes to nature, as a mortal thou couldst not avoid it,—but doubt thou not. Neither "The 5th of May " nor the other sublime works of thy noble mind shall die. They will live eternally to remind thy countrymen of thy revered name.

Inasmuch as the death of MANZONI had been a little misfortune to Italy, on the 7th of June, at a distance only

---

* The poet means to say that a general peace could only be possible after the shedding of much blood should have washed away the crimes produced by so many wars.

of a few days, in Frosinone expired URBANO RATTAZZI. He was born in the year 1808, in Alexandria, consequently he was very nearly 65 years old, and fate, moré friendly to Italy, might have delayed a little longer the awful moment. It pleases me, a son of southern Italy, to praise two sons of the northern provinces. From the Dora and the Po, to Etna and Vesuvius, every city of Italy has furnished her illustrious men, some in arms, some in arts, and others in the sciences. No nation could compete with the numerous phalanx born in our beautiful peninsula.

Leaving aside this digression, which will bring me too far, and which would require a longer time, I come back to Urbano Rattazzi. If Manzoni, as I said just now, was not a member of the militant party,—Rattazzi, instead, for 25 long years, was a member of parliament,—one of the first authors of Italian independence,—and many times the ruler of our destiny. He began his career in the year 1848 and 1849. Defeated at Novara, Piedmont opened its doors to the patriots of Italy; and without fear of mistake, we could assert that from that time Piedmont *was* Italy,—because all the *élite* of the citizens, from the Alps to the sea, had made this province, so deserving, and the cradle of Italian independence, their *rendezvous*.

And here it is worth saying that at that time Rattazzi was second to none; and that all the exiled, who at present are at the head of the Italian nation, found in him a disinterested support and a true patronizing friendship

C

In the year 1859 Count Cavour called Rattazzi to the ministry,—knowing well that by doing so he was working for the good of the country ; disdaining at the same time the indignation aroused against him by the said nomination. This great diplomatist, whose loss Italy will always remember, had understood that, to succeed in his patriotic aspirations, he needed the help of all shades of Liberals, and Rattazzi was one of those patriots more appreciated by him. He clearly showed this by calling him to his death bed, and by choosing him as his successor.

Although Rattazzi,—monarchist, like Cavour,—did not trust in the revolutionary movements, yet he helped the noble General Garibaldi. In the year 1862 and again in 1867 he was the Premier of the Cabinet. Rattazzi, faithful to the dynasty, esteemed by both Charles Albert and Victor Emmanuel, was the leader of that opposition, which, in a constitutional government, is so necessary to elaborate with care the laws, and which is always at hand to take the reins of power whenever the ministry lose the trust and confidence of the nation.

Rattazzi's vote was always in favour of those laws which were useful to Italy. Amongst those are the laws tending to a more complete separation between Church and State. If Manzoni, in his quality as a good patriot apart from the political active field, limited himself to deplore in his heart and in his writings the blindness of a corrupted and traitor clergy, wishing its conversion and repentance, Rattazzi, in his quality as legislator, did all to strip from that party—the real enemy of Italy,—the means to do harm. Do I say *traitor?* This word, to some of you, might seem exaggerated and insulting. Let me, then, declare here before all, that this word is not addressed to those honest men who reconciled the gospel's teachings with the love of their country. Honour to those few! This word, hard as it might seem, is only addressed to those priests who, forgetting to be Italians, uphold all the absurdities which the fancy of the Papal Court dictates. They do not fulfil their mission,—they contaminate the true, the beautiful, the good to support a party which they are pleased to call clerical, and which I think, ought not to exist. Traitors! Yes, traitors and fools. Against those the law will never be severe enough. Would to God that France—this sister nation of Italy—would resolutely enter on the same path, and shake off the yoke of the ecclesiastics, who, in the year 1870, caused her ruin, and who, even to-day, are trying to pull down the present republican institutions, preparing for that unhappy nation new misfortunes and new bloodshed.* The dissension between Italy and France is due to the fanaticism of the French Clergy. The alliance Italo-Prussian, if it exists, and against which I do not dare to speak † is the consequence of the fanaticism of the French-Catholic clergy ; and if Spain does not now find peace, it is only on account of the French fanatic legitimists who en-

---

* Till this year, 1884, the Republic has not yet fallen. A few months after the delivery of this lecture, Gambetta obliged MacMahon to *se soumettre* or *se demettre*. Even in Spain Carlism is quiet.

† Because I find it necessary for the moment, but I do not sympathise with it.

courage their Spanish Carlist brethren. The horizon of the once powerful Latin race is full of dark clouds. God grant that a wind of moderate freedom may give it a beautiful serene.

But I have digressed far from my subject, to which I hasten to return. Rattazzi belongs to that great number of Italians who first imagined the union of Italy under one monarchy,—who consecrated all the strength of their talents, all the energy of their lives, to realize this great dream,—and who finally arrived at Rome, raised on the Capitol the Italian flag, have proved to all the world the falseness of the two insults thrown in the face of Italy by the Austrian diplomatist Metternich, and by the French poet Lamartine. "*Italy is a geographical point,*" said the former; "*Italy is the land of the dead,*" wrote the latter. Thanks to Victor Emmanuel, Cavour, Mazzini, Garibaldi and a thousand others, dead or alive, Italy *is*,— and her tricolor flag commands the respect of all the world.

Rattazzi was not only a good patriot, but he was also a most powerful orator. How many times have I, who speak to you to-night, seen and heard him without being tired, and with increasing pleasure. His words flow easily from his lips. Thin, not endowed with Brofferio's strong voice, he spoke placidly as though he was chattering; and while the Member for Torino would have deserved the name of "impetuous torrent," Rattazzi would have been compared to a sweet and placid stream. If Brofferio persuaded and excited for the moment,—Rattazzi convinced for ever.

In regard to his character, Rattazzi was modest and mild, he knew how to deserve the love even of his political adversaries, and was the bond of union between the two parties. That Italy has felt the importance of this loss, is clearly shown by the voluntary mourning of both houses,—by the king's letters,—by the presence at the funerals of the crown prince,—and of all the patriotic societies ; and the gratitude of a nation toward those deserving it, is not only a proof of the greatness of the nation, but it is also a spur of emulation to the citizens to faithfully discharge their duties.

And here I pause, still moved by grief, making my last remark. Two men, both so precious to Italy, dead at such a short interval! Perhaps at this thought tears are ready to flow from your eyes. Dry them, man must die,—while their deeds remain. You my countrymen may well be proud to add to the many of those who revere the names of Manzoni and Rattazzi. Speak of them to your sons,—narrate to them their deeds and their virtues,—inspire them to imitate the same ; and educate your children so as to be worthy of their country. This is the most sincere wish of my heart ; and this will be the best tribute to the memory of our great men, who from heaven will smile in looking at a new generation of Italians,—worthy of themselves and of their own country.